SKY WOMAN

INDIGENOUS WOMEN WHO HAVE

SHAPED, MOVED OR INSPIRED US

Edited by Sandra Laronde

Library and Archives Canada Cataloguing in Publication

Sky woman : indigenous women who have shaped, moved or
inspired us / editor, Sandra Laronde.

ISBN 1-894778-19-7

1. Indigenous women--Literary collections. 2. Indian art.
I. Laronde, Sandra, 1965-

NX652.W6S59 2005   704'.042   C2005-904710-0

Editor: Sandra Laronde   Theytus Books Ltd.
Text Design: Suzanne Bates   Green Mountain Rd., Lot 45
Cover Design: Maya Gonzalez   RR#2, Site 50, Comp. 8
Copyedit: Andrea Raymond   Penticton, BC, V2A 6J7
                                      Printed in Canada

On behalf of Native Women in the Arts, we would like to extend our appreciation to:
The Millennium Fund at the Canada Council for the Arts
Aboriginal Arts at the Ontario Arts Council
National Aboriginal Achievement Foundation
Casino Rama
Johnson & Johnson

On behalf on Theytus Books, we woould like to acknowledges the support of the following:

We acknowledge the financial support of the Government of Canada through the Book Publishing Industry Development Program (BPIDP) for our publishing activities.

We acknowledge the support of the Canada Council for the Arts which last year invested $20.3 million in writing and publishing throughout Canada.

Nous remercions de son soutien le Conseil des Arts du Canada, qui a investi 20,3 millions de dollars l'an demier dans les lettres et l'édition à travers le Canada.

We acknowledge the support of the Province of the British Columbia through the British Columbia Arts Council.

Sky Woman

Indigenous Women Who Have Shaped, Moved or Inspired Us

Edited by Sandra Laronde

Theytus Books Ltd.

Acknowledgements

Many people participated in the development of this anthology. Foremost, we gratefully acknowledge the 38 women from 22 nations who have contributed their work to make this publication possible. To the Selection Committee who took on a very difficult task: Kim Anderson, Cyndy Baskin, Frances Beaulieu, Sandra Laronde and Kerry Potts.

A special thank you to Anita Large, Andrea Raymond, Suzanne Bates, Greg Young-Ing, Marie-Micheline Hamelin and our collaborating publisher Theytus Books.

Native Women in the Arts
401 Richmond St. West, Suite 420
Toronto, ON
M5V 3A8
416-598-4078
www.nativewomeninthearts.com

Table of Contents

⁺⁺Visual Art⁺⁺

Introduction

Sky Woman is our first woman. She is our mother, our sister, and she is a part of all of us. From Sky Woman springs our ability to create and our ability to dream. She sings out the story of Turtle Island, and our relationship to the sky world, star world, water world, earth world and dream world. She is our connective tissue. She was the first to move, shape and inspire us. She is our first hero.

Earth and creation, as we know it, was born when Sky Woman fell from the stars. According to both the Anishnaabe (Ojibway) and Haudenosaunee (Iroquois) cultures, Sky Woman once lived in the Sky World where earth years were but mere seconds to the Sky People. Sky People were magical beings who were surrounded by a gentle light, and they knew neither pain nor death. They were similar to human beings in their ability to love and care for one another, and in their ability to dream.

Sky Woman fell from the upper world through a hole in the sky. At that time, the world below was made entirely of deep water. Many creatures helped her to descend, but it was one lowly creature that sacrificed his life to ensure her safe landing. When Sky Woman fell from the stars, earth was born.

Since Sky Woman, millions and millions of Indigenous women have inherited her legacy. As Indigenous women, we have been resourceful, resilient and remarkable in our will to keep falling and moving forward. We fall to better ground because of the many women who have gone before us, breaking our fall, and inspiring us from the shining example of their own incandescent lives.

On behalf of Native Women in the Arts, I asked the contributors to write about Indigenous women who have shaped, moved or inspired them. *Sky Woman* is about a fierce respect and reverence for those whose names made history and for the millions whose names did not.

In *Sky Woman*, readers will find recurrent motifs, dreams, and concerns as expressed in memoir, poetry, fiction, and visual art. We hear from different generations who speak from the heart about the many Indigenous women who have helped to shape their lives. In this landmark volume, nearly 40 writers and visual artists are represented from 22 Indigenous nations from across Canada, United States, Mexico, Pacific Islands and Japan.

Published by Theytus Books, in collaboration with Native Women in the Arts, *Sky Woman* celebrates exceptional First Nations, Inuit and Métis women artists. In presenting the work of nearly 200 women to date, Native Women in the Arts continues a unique and national role in publishing and promoting Indigenous women's literature within Canada and throughout other Indigenous territories around the world.

I gratefully acknowledge the writers and visual artists who make this fourth publication possible, without whom *Sky Woman* could not exist. I would also like to extend my gratitude to the many Indigenous women who have gone before us. They have led to artistic and cultural survival as a people.

On a personal note, I would like to dedicate this book to the women and girls in my life: to my loving mother, Barbara Laronde, for everything that she has taught me, and to my nieces Bobbie, Haley, Katie, Sadie, Willow and Jasmine. And to the exceptional men: my late father, Willis Laronde, Fred Blake, Bill Kester, Gad Horowitz, Sonny Moore, George Peshabo, and to my nephews Kiiwedin and Zachariah. All of these people are stars in my sky.

Sandra Laronde

Poetry

JEANNETTE C. ARMSTRONG

Jeannette C. Armstrong is from the Okanagan Nation and was born and raised on the Penticton Reserve. A graduate of the University of Victoria and founder and Executive Director of the En'owkin Centre, she is a renowned visual artist, activist, educator and author. Her articles, essays, oratory, poetry and stories have been anthologized in over 100 publications, and her own titles include *Dancing with the Cranes, Enwhisteetkwa, Neekna and Chemai, Breathtracks, The Native Creative Process,* and *Whispering in Shadows.* She is the editor of a collection of essays entitled *Looking at the Words of Our People: First Nations Analysis of Literature* and co-editor of the *Anthology of Native Poetry in Northern North America.* Her novel, *Slash* is a Canadian bestseller.

BACKGROUND TO JEANNETTE'S ARMSTRONG WATER POEM

As part of the Kyoto International Conference organized by the United Nations Educational, Scientific and Cultural Organization (UNESCO) on March 16, 2003, Jeannette participated in the Opening Plenary of the Third World Water Forum theme of "Water and Cultural Diversity." She was asked to write a "water poem" to share along with her remarks. *Siwlkw*, the water poem, was previously published on UNESCO Canada's website report of the Conference.

JEANNETTE C. ARMSTRONG

Water is Siwlkw

siwlkw
she murmured
is an emergence
following all else
the completeness of the design
in the same instant to become
to be lapped continuously onto long pink tongues
in that breathing to be the sweet drink coursing to become the body
a welling spring eternally renewing
a sacred song of the mother
vibrating outward from the first minute drop formed of sky, earth and light
bursting out of the deep quietness

siwlkw is a song she breathed
awakening cells
toward this knowing that you are the great River
as is the abundant land it brings
to make it's basins, it's fertile plains, it's banks, it's great deltas and estuaries
even to where it finally joins once again
the grandmother ocean's vast and liquid peace
as is the headwater glaciers of the jagged mountains
waiting for the yearly procession of thunder beings
bearing the dark cloud's sweep upward
as spirits
released from green depths cradling whale song
dance on wind
as are the cold ice springs feeding rushing brooks and slow willow draped creeks
meandering through teeming wetlands to sparkling blue lakes
as are the silent underground reservoirs coursing gradually
up toward roots reaching down to draw dew upward through unfurlings into the
sun's full light,
as much as the salmon and sleek sturgeon sliding through strong currents
even the tall straight reeds cleaning stagnant pools
as are the marsh bogs swarming multitudinous glistening flagella and wings in
high country
holding priceless moisture to slowly let it descend through loam and luxuriant life

siwlkw

she said remember this song is the way
it is the storm's way driving new wet earth down slippery slopes to make fresh

land
the river's way heaving its full silt weight crushing solid rock
the tide's way smoothing old beds of stone finally and deciding for all
the way of ice piled green layer upon layer over eons
sustaining this fragment of now so somewhere on her voluptuous body
the rain continues to fall in the right places
the mists unceasingly float upward to where they must
and the fog always ghosts across the land in the cool desert wind where no rain
falls
and each drop is more precious than blood
balancing time in the silvery hoar frost and iridescent ice tinkling under caribou
bellies
her song is the sky's way holding the gossamer filaments of rainbow together
guarding the silent drift of perfect white flakes where the moose stop momentarily
to look upward
it is her song in the forest
ensuring a leaf shaped just so
captures the glistening droplets
and pumps through the veins of the lion parting undulating grasses
and lifts from the ground in great Condor wings soaring last circles in the
mountains of Chile
to the places it moves in subterranean caverns through porous stone
seeping and wetting sand deep down
released to caress smooth pebbles.

This song is the way

• • • •

KATHY AINSLEY

Kathy Ainsley (Seneca/Dutch) is a poet and artist. She is a member of Wordcraft Circle of Native Writers and Storytellers and has worked as an art teacher and for *Mothering Magazine*. She has one son, Galen, who is also an artist, and she currently resides in the Santa Cruz Mountains with her husband Harry.

Ancestral Harvest

In the Seneca creation story, Sky Woman falls from the upper world through a hole in the sky. The world below is made entirely of water. The animals see her hurling toward the deep waters and are concerned for the strange creature. Remembering that there is earth at the bottom of water, muskrat brings up enough earth to rub onto turtle's back. All at once the earth and turtle become enormous, and Sky Woman lands safely upon the newly created island.

Planting

Sky Woman lands on the eve of the Twenty-First Century.
Concrete has replaced muskrat's gift of mud.
Her seed bag is filled with the women who will come after her.
Blackbirds perch in the ancestral trees of the upper world
back and forth they answer each other in layers of language,
evoking memories in the world below.
A soft wind begins to stir. A hole is opening in the sky.

Tending

Grandmother Effie is carefully being led by the arm to her granddaughter.
Her eyes no longer perceive images in the world below the sky.
To this old woman's hand the girl feels beautiful with her deep set eyes
and short strong body. Reminded of the daughter she has outlived,
the circle of her life floats upward, entering a hole in the sky.

The Harvest

All of my grandmother's fallen remains are the sacred earth and water
that surround Turtle Island. Each generation catches the next Sky Woman's
fall. My Mother is strong earth. She weaves the legacy of woman and

earth together, forming new landscape.
Every daughter inherits this legacy as her birthright.
Every daughter begins as Sky Woman and every daughter will become
Old Woman.
Every daughter will catch the fall of the next and every daughter will fall.
Every daughter will harvest her crop and return to seed again.
And for every daughter the sky will open once more.

••••

CATHERINE McCARTY

Catherine McCarty is an Ojibway of mixed blood, from Nipissing First Nation in North Bay, Ontario. She has been working as a nurse since 1987, and is a single mother of a 14-year-old daughter, Kachina.

Cathy has had her poems published by *Native Beat* newspaper, *in a vast dreaming* (Native Women in the Arts), *The International Library of Poetry*, and the *Poetry Institute of Canada*, where she received an Award of Excellence in 2000/2001, for her writings.

"Let us celebrate that we, as Aboriginal women, have been able to live on and into the new millennium - due to the perseverance of our grandmothers. They understood and accepted consequences, and still continued to pass on traditions to ensure the future of our birthrights and cultures today."

CATHERINE McCARTY

Our Grandmothers

They spoke of tribes, no one has ever heard about
Sang songs people said made no sense
Celebrated in ceremonies that were desecrated
Held on to traditions and prophecies, politicians won't ever understand
Brought back what was destroyed and told it never existed

When speaking of truth, were alienated
Stood up for themselves, then threatened
Refused to change their name and given a number
Grew their hair long and forced to cut it

Spoke their own language and were beaten
Died unknowingly, and told they had it coming
Wanted freedom, but needed authorization
Crossed the line and were persecuted

They've seen their brother's scalps in museums
Sacred belongings and clothing at auctions
Continued to dance and dress from their days
And saw their designs bring profit
They've watched society make wealth from their land and resources
Honoured all treaties and saw them diminish
Asked for self government and new constitutions were written
And have the Great Law ignored

They are all my relations, the countless gone, but never forgotten
The lifelines of our people you met centuries ago
A nation that endured, the proud women, you called "Indians"

····

NICOLA CAMPBELL

Nicola Campbell is from the Nicola Valley in British Columbia. She is
Interior Salish, of Thompson and Okanagan ancestry on her mother's side, and
Métis on her father's side. She is completing a Bachelor's of Fine Arts in Creative
Writing and First Nations Studies at the University of British Columbia. Her first
children's book will be released in fall 2005.

Buckle Up Shoes

She'd twirl by herself
in the living room
to the Beatles
and Wanda Jackson,

when she thought no one was watching.
I'd peek around the corner
4 feet tall maybe with moccasins on
and whispy braids.

Tired out from a day full of
play
I'd watch her feet
Remembering

In black buckle up shoes,
a skirt with flare,
a red blouse with a pretty collar,
auburn hair in curls,

Old Mom twirling
like a little girl.

NICOLA CAMPBELL

lullabies

So many nights i sat awake
and listened
      Old Mom
      you were speaking
      Nle7kepmxcin
      speaking
      Nsilxcin
with the many old ones
who came through the door.

i sat quietly sometimes
sometimes pestering you
      with questions

belly warm with
      toast,
      hot tea,
      pacific cream
      and sugar.

i traced designs
with my fingers on the

red and white table cloth
black and white benches.

listening carefully to every word
you said.
calmed by gentle rhythms of
grandmother voices
and stories only heard
in the quiet hours
between Elders.

••••

QWO-LI DRISKILL

Qwo-Li Driskill is Cherokee Two-Spirit also of African, Irish, Lenape and Osage descent. Her work has appeared in numerous publications including *Revolutionary Voices: A Multicultural Queer Youth Anthology*, *Many Mountains Moving* and *The Evergreen Chronicles* and will soon be appearing in the anthology *Speak to Me Words*. An activist, poet and educator, Qwo-Li lives in the Duwamish Nation in Seattle, Washington, where she is the founder of Knitbone Productions: A First Nations Ensemble.

Beginning Cherokee

Tal'-s-go Gal'-quo-gi Di-del'-qua-s-do-di Tsa-la-gi Di-go-whe-li/ Beginning Cherokee

I-gv-yi-i Tsa-la-gi Go-whe-lv-i: A-sgo-hni-ho-'i/
First Cherokee Lesson: Mourning

> Find a flint blade
> Use your teeth as a whetstone
> Cut your hair
> Talk to shadows and crows
> Cry your red throat raw
> Learn how to translate the words you miss most:
> *dust*   *love*   *poetry*
> *Learn to say*   *home*
>
> My cracked earth lips
> drip words not sung
> as lullabies to my infant ears
> not laughed over dinner
> or choked on in despair
> No
>
> They played dead until
> the soldiers passed
> covered the fields like corpses
> and escaped further into the mountains
> *When it's safe we'll find you*
> they promised
> But we were already gone

before sunrise

I crawl through piles of
Twisted bodies to find them
I do everything *Beginning Cherokee*
tells me
Train my tongue
to lay still
Keep teeth tight
against lips
listen to instruction tapes
study flash cards

How can I greet my ancestors in a language they don't understand

My tear ducts fill with milk
because what I love most
was lost at birth

My blood roars skin to blisters
weeps haunted calls of owls
bones splinter
jut through skin
until all of me is wounded
as this tongue

Ta-li-ne-i Tsa-la-gi Go-whe-lv-I: A-ni-sgi-li/
Second Cherokee Lesson: Ghosts

> Leave your hair
> at the foot of your bed
> Scratch your tongue
> with a cricket's claw to speak again
> Stop the blood with cornmeal

> Your ancestors will surround you as you sleep
> Keep away ghosts of generals presidents priests
> who hunger for your
> rare and tender tongue
> They will keep away ghosts
> so you have strength
> to battle the living

Stories float through lives
with an owl's sudden swooping

I knew some Cherokee
when I was little
My cousins taught me
My mother watches it all happen again
sees ghosts rush at our throats
with talons drawn like bayonets
When I came home speaking
your grandmother told me
I forbid you to speak that language
in my house
Learn something useful

We sit at the kitchen table
As she drinks iced tea
in the middle of winter
I teach her to say u-ga-lo-ga-tlv-tv-nv/ tea
across buckets of peanut butter
wonder break diet coke
Try to teach her something useful

I am haunted by loss
My stomach is a knot of serpents
and my hair grows out
as owl feathers

Tso-i-ne-i Tsa-la-gi Go-whe-lv-i: Anvdadisdi/
Third Cherokee Lesson: Memory

      Raid archeologists' camps
      and steal shovels
      to rebury the dead
      Gather stores like harvest
      and sing honour songs
      Save the seeds
      to carry you through the winter
      Bury them deep in your flesh
      Weep into your palms
      until stories take root
      in your bones
      split skin
      blossom

There are stories caught
in my mother's hair
I can't bear the weight of

Could you give me a braid
straight down the middle
of my back just the way I like
So I part her black-going-silver hair
into three strands
thick as our history
radiant as crow wings

This is what it means to be Indian
Begging for stores in a living room
stacked high with newspapers magazines baby toys

Mama story me

She remembers
        Great Grandmother Nancy Harmon
        who heard white women
        call her uppity Indian during
        a quilting bee
        and climbed down their chimney with
        a knife between her teeth

She remembers
        Flour sack dresses
        tar paper shacks
        dust storms   blood   escape

She remembers so I can

She carries fire on her back
My fingers work swiftly as spiders
and the words that beat in my throat
are dragonflies

She passes stories down to me
and because I am the one
taking back our tongue
I pass words up to her
Braid her hair

It's what she doesn't say
that could destroy me
what she can't say
She weeps milk

14

Nv-gi-ne-i Tsa-la-gi Go-whe-lv-i: U-de-nv/
Fourth Cherokee Lesson: Birth

> Gather riverbank clay
> to make a bowl
> Fill it with hot tears
> Strap it to your back
> with spider silk
>
> Keep your flint knife close
> to ward off death
> and slice through umbilical cords
> Be prepared for blood

Born without a womb
I wait for the crown of fire
the point where further stretching is impossible
This birth could split me
I gently nudge each syllable into movement
Memorize their smells
Listen to their strange sleepy sounds
They shriek with hunger and loss
so I hold them to my chest and weep milk
because my breasts are filled with tears

I wrap my hair around their small bodies
a river of owl feathers

See they whisper *We found you*
We made a promise

This time we'll be more careful
Not lose each other in
the chaos of slaughter

We are together at sunrise
from dust we sprout love and poetry
We are home
Greeting our ancestors
With rare and tender tongues

• • • •

JESSIE HOUSTY

Jessie Housty is an 18-year-old Heiltsuk woman living on the central raincoast of British Columbia. She has been writing poetry for a number of years and is inspired by the depth and beauty of her culture and the place that she lives. She has also found inspiration in the many incredible Aboriginal women who have acted as mentors and role models for her as she grew to become a woman herself.

POTLACH SERIES - POEM IV

weaving cries
from deep red bark,
curving boughs
of power
rising with the footsteps
of the dancer -
her brow adorned
with rings of cedar
where honour bears witness
to these rites

WITNESS TO THIS BIRTH

she slips the sunrise
around her bare brown shoulders
to dance for this newborn babe.
her feet become grace,
her movements become beauty
and her spirit names this child Morning.
silent hymns of a dawn
baptized by ocean and sky:
these become her every breath.
the earth in her skin is awoken
and wrapped in the sun;
this infancy lasts not long
though it is bound in glory.
with a bow of her head,
she honours creation.

JESSIE HOUSTY

LITTLE BEAR

her lips graze the petals of dawn's rebirth -
the sky naked, vulnerable in the
salmon-pink blush of youth and innocence.
as the trees trace beauty along the horizon,
she presses her voice against the breath of the wind,
caressing it with her quiet song.
she walks until her feet reach the distance, then rests -
dipping her hands into pools of light
and laughing with the shadows that dance
at the command of her fingertips.
she sleeps in the arms of the afternoon,
her breathing a kiss for the ocean and the rain,
awakening only to frolic with the night.
she plays in the rivers of light
trickling from the stars, and waits patiently
by the side of the moon
for morning to swoop down and carry her away once more.

••••

JANE INYALLIE

Jane Inyallie is Tse'khene from McLeod Lake, British Columbia (B.C.), and currently lives in Vanderhoof B.C. with her partner Gayle, their two dogs, Xena and Poncho, donkey Chimo and goat Smokey. They spend their summers hiking, walking, and camping with Xena and Poncho.

salmon bone woman

a voice calls to me
in the daytime of my dreams

words turn to patterns
charming me with colours
wrap me in layers
muffling everyday sounds

i am taken to an unknown place
people with flattened heads
broken legs and twisted limbs
stand in silence

i look into sunken eyes
misshapen skulls covered
by overhanging hoods

heads turn to me
with skin smoothed over
one or both eyes

i wonder
how this could be
turn to look back
everything disappears

a few children run by
with laughter and smiles

sunshine brings
salmon bone woman
who comes from

a land beneath the sea

we sit and talk
over bannock and tea

when she is gone
i find bundles of salt
and a carved bone
i wear at the base of my throat

when i sing
i hear a voice
it belongs to
salmon bone woman
who comes from
a land beneath the sea

For Deborah

••••

NEHI KATAWASISIW

Nehi Katawasisiw was born and raised in northern Manitoba, but she calls both Saskatchewan where her father (Plains Cree) is from, and Manitoba where her mother (Swampy Cree and Saulteaux) is from, home.

In 1999, Nehi moved to Santa Fe, New Mexico where she attended the Institute of American Indian Arts and majored in Creative Writing and Fine Art. She graduated in 2002 with an Associate of Arts degree. She is currently at Smith College in Massachusetts where she is studying Sociology and Anthropology with a minor in International Relations; she will graduate in 2005.

Nehi's main interests revolve around the issues of international de-colonization efforts, self-determination and sovereignty, as well as post-colonial cultural continuity. Her work in writing and visual art are narratives of the experience of belonging to a nation whose lands are colonized, and the heart of that experience, which is deeply rooted in an Indigenous philosophy.

moccasins c. 1880

they stand there together
and empty of the feet that made them walk
who wore them, these circa moccasins
which ancestor trod the earth in these
beaded
tanned
buffalo
shoes
they carry the imprints of unknown feet
maybe a relative of mine, from the circa past
wore them through the pining forest trees,
across the rippling lowering plain
hunting
invisible
buffalo
hides
whose sweat and pain and joy
entered those isolated moccasin shoes
whose floral motif decries the 'savage'
indelicate hands that stitched so carefully
tender

pain
taking
hands
there they stand, those circa moccasins
kept behind that glass, imprisoned within it
still not free, not since circa 1880
when the walls were glass and pining trees

KOKUM'S HAIR

My *kokum's* skin in afternoon light;
      like onion paper
written on with ripples traces of muskeg moon
      and bitterroot snow.

My *kokum* sits in her chair
      beads and feathers arrayed around her
unsewn fan waits for air
      to carry it to the sun.

Her hair, curled and iron grey.
Tells its stories in a tongue I cannot speak,
songs I *can* not sing;
Like words of water teasing moss-bank reeds.

And when I touch her skin like onion paper
My fingertips remember moose hide houses
And how they bled when they sewed,
Their flesh pierced through with a bone tipped awl.

My *kokum's* needles clicking;
      sound of glacier lake rocks shifting
they grow the shape of shores
      from *kona* ice chipped shoulders.

My *kokum's* hair like sinew threads
      braided to her skull
a crown to hold her head up high
      when winter's sons come calling.

                • • • •

BEVERLEE A. PETTIT

A member of the Wyandotte Tribe of Oklahoma, Beverlee Pettit is the daughter of Myrtle Elizabeth Tussinger and granddaughter of Susie Bearskin. Born in Tahlequah, Oklahoma, she came home with her mother and lived in a small, one-room cabin along the Illinois River outside of town. In the ancient corridors of her mind, she remembers the voice of her mother singing lullabies as she lay in a cradle hanging from the limb of a tree near the winding river.

Although Beverlee dropped out of school and worked many odd jobs in her teenage years, she finally settled in a career with the Bureau of Indian Affairs where she climbed the job ladder for 13 years beginning in Albuquerque, New Mexico, then traveling to Northern California, and ending in Arizona with the Colorado River Indian Tribes.

Beverlee loved working with the various Indian tribes, however, she sought more in her profession and obtained a position in the Indian Health Service in Anchorage, Alaska, where she spent eight years increasing her knowledge of the federal sectors that serve the American Indian and Alaska native peoples. Beverlee still felt she needed more and so obtained a position outside of the federal sector with an Alaska Native non-profit health organization where she is now the Director of Human Resources. She has an Associate of Arts degree and is near receiving her Bachelor of Arts in Organizational Management.

With a love for song writing, music, poetry, and short stories, Beverlee continues to strive for a balance of her public and private life in order to be an example for all Native women.

BEVERLEE A. PETTIT

Her Face Fills My Eyes

I am five years old and
she fastened the strings
of the hood
under my chin.
She looks at me and her face fills my eyes.
My whole world is in her face.
Her eyes are my shelter,
Her mouth my love and rebuke,
Her cheeks my comfort,
Her brow my warning,
Her face
The strength of my life
My mother,
Myrtle Elizabeth

••••

RAFAELA PERALES

Rafaela Black Hawk Perales is of Apache and Tahumara ancestry. She is a 52-year-old single mother of one son, and grandmother of two granddaughters. She was born and raised in Southern California, lived in northern Idaho and currently resides in Arizona. She has written poems and short stories for the past 43 years. Being disabled for the last 15 years, has allowed her to indulge in her passion, writing. Recently, she has written a children's book entitled, *The Talking Totem Pole Stories*.

Her poems are the passions of her spirit. She is blessed to often step into others' moccasins and speak for those she calls the voiceless: those who cry out to what too often seems like an uncaring world. In giving voice to her heart and spirit, she also writes poems that express her pain and joy, laughter and tears.

Niña de la Tierra

Yo soy una niña de le tierra.
I am a daughter of the earth.
I carry within my soul the
memory of life and birth.

Yo soy una niña del cielo.
I am a daughter of the sky.
I give my dreams wings, dropping
feathers of hope for those with
shattered lives.

Yo soy una niña de los mares.
I am a daughter of the seas.
I sing away your sorrows and
pain with ancient melodies.

Yo soy una niña de sol.
I am a daughter of the sun.
I light the way through the
darkness for the children
yet to come.

••••

MARCIE RENDON

Marcie Rendon is a mother, grandmother, freelance writer, and sometimes performance artist of White Earth Anishinabe descent. A published writer of poems, songs, short stories, and plays, she was a 1998/1999 recipient of the St. Paul Company's Leadership in Neighborhoods Grant, which strives to create a viable Native presence in the Twin Cities theatre community. Currently a core member of the Playwright Centre, Marcie received a 1996/1997 Jerome Fellowship from the Minneapolis Playwright's Centre. Her first children's book, *Pow Wow Summer*, was published by Carol Rhoda in 1996 and her second book, *The Farmer's Market/ Families Working Together*, was released in February 2001.

a common misconception...

a common misconception
is the assumption
that god created
flowers on a
higher
plane
than
dirt

or say...
tornadoes

my mother
never rode on horses
she ran
with
mustangs

one time
a
tornado
touched
down
saw
her
and
retreated

back
from
where
it
came

another
time
a man
decided
to drink
his fill
of
her

she
washed
his
eyes
out
with
bleach

they
left
her lying
naked
on the
bar room
floor
her
laughter
drove
them
crazy

my father
couldn't
hold
her
she
pinned
him

to
the
sky

while
she
hitch
hiked
cross
the
country
he
let them
take
his
pride

her
body ravaged,
alcohol
t.b.
-they
say-,
she
jumped
the prison
wall

the
wind
never
blessed
her
back
she passed
salmon
on their
way
to spawn
it was
always
too hot
so
she

never
did
come in
from
the
cold

her final
blanket
a
Montana
snowfall

yes
god
created
man
in
his
own
image

woman
made
her
own

. . . .

APRIL A. SEVERIN

April A. Severin is the author of five chapbooks including *Animal Appeal* and *Feast*. Other publishing credits include poetry in *Gatherings, Volume XII: The En'owkin Journal of First North American Peoples* and *Healing Journey*. April reads at many literary and community events throughout Ontario.

Be Who You Are

"Call out my name and my spirit will answer.
I am Ongwehonweh, be who you are."
- ElizaBeth Hill, "The Tobacco Song"

Six Nations
Fall Fair
you sang
strong and proud
rain fell from
April eyes

For me a fair day
you called out my song
my spirit answered
Nia:weh
Ongwehonweh
Be who you are

••••

ARDITH WALKEM

Ardith (Wel-pet'ko We-Dalks) Walkem is a Nlaka'pamux woman from Spence's Bridge in the interior of British Columbia. She is a lawyer who works on Indigenous Peoples' land and resource rights and is currently completing a Masters of Law degree through which she explores the use of Indigenous Peoples' oral traditions as evidence in Canadian courts. She is the co-editor of a book that explores the impact on Indigenous peoples' rights on the constitutionalization of Aboriginal Title and Rights, entitled *Box of Treasures or Empty Box? Twenty Years of Section 35* *(2003)*.

What she did for Indian Government

"The things I've done for Indian Government," she says
and her eyes are black like stones burnt to charcoal
hewn tough in the ashes of a great fire, these eyes can
carry enough heat to bring life for the people to feast again.

There was the time in her younger days when a conspiracy
lurked around every corner, and she answered readily the call
"Rent a white car.
Don't tell anyone where you are going or what you are doing."
She could not, because she did
not know herself.
"Drive the car to the parking lot of the Blue Boy hotel. Park there.
A cowboy will come out of the lobby, take him with you.
Hide him, remember, tell no one."

One of her first strikes for International Indigenous activism.
He was a Sami man who had escaped from Norway
after attempting to bomb a dam, which would have
flooded the reindeer grounds of his people.

When the leaders were scared
She exasperated exploded into action
"If they're too chickenshit, I'll take him"
She hid him and then took him and his family home
to live with her three kids in a small apartment.

She lives the phrase most only wear on buttons pinned
To their jacket lapels

"Indian Rights for Indian Land. Take a Stand"

Scooping a Styrofoam cup full of dirt
into her handbag, together with the mints and candies,
slipping into a press conference where politicians and business leaders
deliver the news of their plans to develop the lands and trees
stolen from Indian people.

The only Indian in attendance.
She marched to the front of the room, past television cameras,
men in suits and ties,
dumped the cupful of soil onto the front table,
"You take this,"
she said
"that's the only scrap of Indian land you're going to get."
Then she turned and marched out, taking the television cameras with her.

During the Constitutional Express to Ottawa
Indians from across the country gathered to demand
recognition and inclusion of our rights in the Canadian constitution.
There was a deadlock,
When it did not seem that the rights were going anywhere,
Events and the airline industry conspired together to break the issue open.
There was only enough money to buy her a one-way ticket to Ottawa,
the Premiere of the Province of B.C. was booked in the economy seats
on her flight right across from her.

She waited while he visited friends in first class,
and then lifted from him the Contents of a binder entitled
"Confidential:
Position Paper of the Province of British Columbia
on Aboriginal People and Constitutional Reform."
Lawyers and Chiefs were conscripted
to distract the Premiere for the rest of the flight
so he would not revisit his empty binder.
She sat innocently and read her book on Ghandi and peaceful resistance.

Before she came south she worked in the friendship centres
of northern towns, and would cajole staff and executives
into vans on bitterly cold nights for a patrol of the streets
where she would pick up the people who were too drunk to know
to come in from the cold. She would break zoning bylaws
and insurance contracts because none of these
meant anything if you left your people cold and defenseless
on the streets.

She is the woman who visits college campus auditoriums
and church basements to speak with anyone who will listen
and the spirits walk with her, place
their hands on her shoulders to urge her onwards.
There are times, when eagles come to soar
outside windows when she speaks.

"You have to believe," she advises the young people
who come to her, and ask her how to find a voice
for the people, for the land
*"You have to feel. Because if you can feel, you
can make other people feel and that's what matters."*

There were the times later when she had acquired the nickname
"Mother of the People."
Emblazoned bold on the aprons
made to costume her for the pancake breakfasts
she would supervise to nurture the people come to
talk around campfires about the land. She was from Old Crow
but the idea of putting "Old Crow" on the apron was discarded
out of fear that the breakfasters might take this for her nickname
and be treated to an unholy fury, although she laughed in private.

For all that her instincts unerringly guide us in the ways of
government, we learned early
that her instincts while driving were not so honed.
Rooted in the times before cars and highways,
she was built to walk upon the land and in the
hearts of the people.
Her instincts befuddled when faced with automobiles and asphalt.

After a six-hour drive to Lillooet, she would stare in
astounded amazement at the city limit sign welcoming
her to Kamloops
"Kamloops??! Kamloops??!" she would look about the car
in amazement, to see if anyone else had been in on the trick
"How'd we get to Kamloops??"

She has retired three times,
but only to get a change of scenery
because she cannot bear to sit at home
bake cookies or attend tea socials,
when there might be a new government plan
being carried forward.
She plots the next revolution, the carrying forward of the Indian

movement in restaurant booths and over telephone wires.

"Those people…"
is her rallying cry to battle,
and when she turns to stride forward throwing only
a *"Come"* over her shoulder,
grown women who she has dubbed *"the Kids"* know she means them, and
follow behind her.

True leaders walk with the people,
cook for the people,
theirs may not be the stories recorded in history books,
or archived in the vaults of newspapers, but
for all that she has done for Indian Government
she is one of the only true leaders we have ever met.

• • • •

Short Stories

SALLY-JO BOWMAN

Sally is Native Hawaiian from Kailua, O'ahu and is a descendant of the Pa family of the Puna and Hilo districts of the Big Island of Hawaii. In the last 17 years, she has used her talent for writing to create an awareness of her people throughout the world by writing about their culture and history. Over a quarter of her 200 published works are written about Native Hawaiian subjects. In 2002, her first poem was published in *Oiwi*, a Native journal, along with a chapter from her novel-in-progress, which deals with the fall of the monarchy in Hawaii in 1893, a trauma so deep the wounds are still fresh after 100 years. Many Hawaiian women and Native North American woman have profoundly influenced Sally, and Auntie Betty, from *Voice of the Beloved*, is among them.

Voice of the Beloved

The morning Ku and Hina joined, I knelt in the low-tide, reef-protected shallows of Mokule'ia with my sandals cast on to the dry sand and my skirt hiked around my hips. My inappropriate dress testified that I had not expected an encounter with the ocean – or with a gourd, or with "Mama," kupuna Betty Jenkins' 90-year-old mother, Elizabeth Ellis.

I was not thinking of the progenitor Hawaiian gods, the archetype male and female. My purpose was to learn more about the kupuna role at the Office of Hawaiian Affairs. Auntie Betty had invited me to a cultural workshop for Office of Hawaiian Affairs staff members that she was holding at her beachside home. I expected motivation and morale building. You know, a pep talk about the good of the organization and the glory of being a corporate cog.

I had met the gracious Auntie Betty once before so I should have known there would be a twist; I should have known that my status as an observer would last barely minutes.

My first clue should have been the name of her home: Kai Hawanawana, "Whispering Sea." Then, I spotted 30 or so dry-but-dirty gourds sitting on her rain-washed lawn.

"Nana ka maka," Auntie Betty said to 20 assembled employees and me. "Look at these ipu. They have had a hard life. They've been exposed to rain and sun and they are covered with dirt and mold. But listen to them. One will call to you. Do not pick one up and put it down to choose another. Let one call. Ho'olohe. Obey."

When nearly everyone else had taken one, I walked slowly to the band of gourds. Of the remaining eight, one with a fat neck seemed like a child in need of love. I picked it up.

"Ho'oma'ema'e me ke kai," Auntie Betty said. It is time for cleansing the sea.

We walked our gray and dismal looking gourds down a slope of course sand. I strapped my watch to my tank top, hitched up my skirt, and knelt at the water's edge, following instructions, with the others scouring the scum from my ipu with limu and sand.

All the ipu began to shine, the hidden beauty of gold and brown coming out as if it were the kaona, the "veiled meaning," of a Hawaiian chant or song. Women called to each other, holding their gourds up and turning them, "Look! Nice, yeah?"

I worked and worked in the morning sun with the quiet water lapping, whispering, Kai hawanawana. I scrubbed away at the bottom, the rounded sides, the neck, and around the stem, which was as withered as a baby's umbilical cord ready to fall off.

When we finished, we walked back to the house.

"How beautifully we shine when someone cares for us," Auntie Betty said. "Keep listening to your ipu. It will tell you its name."

I listened as I took my ipu through the next steps. Ka 'oki'ana, cut the neck. Ho'oma'ema'e na'au, clean the inside, the guts. But save the seeds.

The neck was big enough that I could get my hand inside the gourd. I pulled at its dusty, dried fibres. I think I heard a small whisper, like the whisper of the sea, perhaps the rattle of seeds still bound in the stringy membrane within. The voice said, "Pilialoha," beloved.

I thumped the gourd's bottom to loosen the last seeds. The sound was firm and mellow.

"Nice sound," another woman said.

"Ka Leo," I thought, "The Voice."

The next step was Ha'awi iona i ka ipu, "Naming the gourd." With a formal title for the process, I know this wasn't the time to casually write the word on the bottom of the gourd with a Magic Marker. The name would bring mana, the life force, living power.

"I'm ready," I said to Auntie Betty.

"Talk to Mama," she said.

Mama sat in the house, a tiny wisp of a Chinese-Hawaiian woman in a soft mu'umu'u. I knelt at her side with the shining, golden gourd. I feared that my paltry knowledge of Hawaiian language was so inadequate that I might accidentally give my gourd a name with a dark meaning.

"What name do you think?" Mama said.

"Pilialoha. It is from the name of my home, Hale Pilialoha."

"Beloved," Mama said. "A good name."

"I think there's more. More came to me." I paused. I wasn't sure of my Hawaiian grammar. Maybe the rest was too stupid, or simple or presumptuous. "Ka Leo," I said. "May I call it Kaleopilialoha?" Had I really heard these words before or was this wishful thinking? My heart thumped beneath my ribs as if it were inside the gourd. I did not want to be dubbed a fool.

"Yes," Mama said, her gentle milky old eyes looking right into mine. "Yes, that is good. The voice of the beloved."

Auntie Betty had said the ancient people used gourds for dozens of purposes: to store things in, to carry water, to keep the rhythm of chants and songs. Are we not like gourds, to serve many purposes? Must we not cleanse ourselves inside and out to be able to do our work? When we have done all this in the right order, must we not be beautiful? The corporate pep talk was over.

The next morning I took Kaleopilialoha to the beach of my own babyhood, to the morning surf of Kailua. We sang together, Kaleo and I, knee-deep in the chop and backwash of the incoming tide, chanting what Auntie Betty had taught:

E ho mai

E ho mai

E ho mai ka 'ike mai e

O na mea huna no'eau o na mele e

E ho mai

E ho mai

E ho mai ka 'ike mai e.

Guide us from above. Help us to know the hidden meaning of the chant. Thump-thump, thump thump thump, Kaleo kept the cadence. I splashed the gourd with water. The sea, or the sky, or the spirits compelled me to talk to it. "You were born in salt water, as was I. You seem to be male, for I am female. We are all both male and female, Ku and Hina. I am the Path of The Rainbow, Keala-o-Anuenue. But I must also be you, a voice. You were born yesterday, Kaleopilialoha, at Mokule'ia. Today I honor you at my own beloved Kailua. You shall give full voice to E Ho Mai. Guide us from above. Show us the hidden meaning of the chant."

Here I was, talking to a gourd, but I didn't care if people taking their morning beach walk thought I was lolo.

I remembered Kai Hawanawana, the Whispering Sea. At the end of the morning at Mokule'ia, Auntie Betty had hugged me. "I see that you 'got it,'" she said. She held me at arm's length, smiling. And she whispered like the sea, "The gourd is you."

•••

CHISATO O. DUBREUIL

Born in northern Japan to an Ainu woman and a Japanese man, Chisato Dubreuil moved to North America in 1985. After graduating with a Bachelor of Arts and a Master of Arts in Native Art History of First Nations people of British Columbia's Northwest Coast, she accepted a position with the Smithsonian Institute in Washington, D.C. to co-curate a major exhibition on the art and culture of the Ainu. She also wrote and co-edited with Fitzhugh and Dubreuil a major book, *Ainu: Spirit of a Northern People*, (University of Washington Press, 1999). Currently finishing a PhD at the University of Victoria, Chisato continues to publish and speak on Ainu, Japanese, and Northwest Coast art and culture, and is finishing a monograph on the life and art of the gifted Ainu sculptor, Bikky Sunazawa (1931-1989).

Her Name is Peramonkoro!

The greatest treasures of any Aboriginal culture are its elders. The men and women who give to their culture the gifts of evolving traditions allow us to survive as a people. Some of the most important of these gifts are the various creative expressions found in the arts. Today there is a growing body of scholarly work devoted to Aboriginal art, the *things* that become the icons of the Aboriginal culture. Even though both men and women made traditional art, it was the creative efforts of women that people often identified with, for example, pottery, basketry, blanket making, and beadwork. While Native women are credited for the creation of traditional works of art, little credit is given to those women artists who are also cultural leaders. Of course, we who identify with an Aboriginal culture know it is the women who are at the centre of our universe. For those of us fortunate enough to find some measure of success, it is often a special woman who helped get us there.

I am Ainu, the indigenous people of northern Japan. My continuing inspiration is from an Ainu woman who was born in 1897. I never met her but her legacy is the stuff of legends, and her leadership, even from the grave, continues to provide me, and so many others, the positive qualities needed to reach our potential. Her life was hard, not simply because she was Native woman, but also because of personal life choices made because of her strength of character.

The Ainu lost all the wars, and our territory, to Japan by 1800. As with all Native cultures, the victorious foreign invader immediately set out to systematically destroy the culture. Because of Hokkaido's harsh winters and rugged wilderness, the Japanese takeover was slow. They first concentrated on taking control of the wild food source, particularly the salmon, which was as important to the Ainu as they are to the Aboriginal people of British Columbia, and then they started to dismantle the Ainu culture. For example, in 1875, the Japanese banned the practice of naming an Ainu child with an Ainu name.

Although the Ainu lost their independence, they were not a defeated people. Many Ainu practiced individual acts of passive resistance. In traditional times, a newly born child was not given a *proper* Ainu name until the age of seven or eight. In July of 1896, a young Ainu woman, Utepanka, found herself pregnant. She and her husband, Kosonku, were thrilled to start their family, and on March 6, 1897, their daughter was born and given a temporary name.

However, as the time approached to give their daughter her lasting name, her mother and father decided they just could not give her a Japanese name. Their daughter was Ainu and they never wanted her to forget her heritage, and they proudly announced, "Her name is Peramonkoro!" meaning "child playing with a spatula." While the name has a domestic ring to it, she would use it as badge of honour, a statement of her Ainuness. It was a name the Japanese wished they had never heard, and one they would not soon forget.

Unfortunately, little of her early years were recorded. At the time, the grade school system was segregated because the Japanese believed that Ainu children were not intellectual equals with the Japanese, and the quality of Ainu education initially amounted to little more than instruction on the Japanese language and other products of forced assimilation. Even with the substandard education, the intellect of Peramonkoro was formidable. The Ainu of the time experienced dramatic discrimination and all were extremely poor. When you were poor and Native, getting an education was always a problem. For example, the Japanese high school system demanded everyone wear a specific type of kimono, a uniform that was a very expensive item for the Ainu. However, Peramonkoro's family was determined that she receive a good education. They worked tirelessly to buy the kimono, and she went to school. While Peramonkoro excelled at school, her parents' dream of education bringing equality died a quick death. Discrimination, a fact of like for all Native people, was too strong.

After graduating, her attempts at finding a position to match her intellect were futile. With no chance of a *professional* life, she married because it was a cultural expectation. She married a good, but strong willed, Ainu man. Taught to never settle for less than her potential, Peramonkoro's formative years gave her an air of independence that clashed with her husband's equally independent attitude. While there was mutual respect, neither was happy and they divorced, but remained friends throughout their lives. In the 1920s, divorce in Japan was extremely rare, carrying with it severe social stigma. The divorce was a major decision, not something that she was proud of, but something she felt she had to do. Undeterred, she moved on with her life and married another strong willed, Ainu man by the name of Koakanno Sunazawa. This time, the personalities were an excellent match, driven by a mutual sense of purpose.

In the 1920s, Peramonkoro braved many challenges, the first of which offended the Japanese sensitivities when she publicly rejected the Japanese-held belief that the emperor, Hirohito, was a divine figure. While Peramonkoro never wavered in the traditional Ainu belief that all manner of things had a *kamuy*, a good spirit, she was exposed to Christianity and embraced those tenets that she felt gave her strength. More than a private belief, she opened her home to other Ainu for Sunday school services and often invited Salvation Army officers to join them. While most Ainu gravitated toward Buddhism, more or less the national religion of Japan, she maintained her special spirituality throughout her life. While divorced Ainu were rare, those holding any Christian beliefs, especially publicly stated, were truly unique.

Challenging the Japanese theology was one thing, challenging them over land issues, which were always at the core of any Native/non-Native dialogue, required real courage considering many Ainu lost their lives fighting for their land in earlier years. Refusing to accept the constant illegal appropriation of Ainu land by the Japanese invader, Peramonkoro, along with her husband and infant son, Bikky, joined three others in extended trips to Tokyo, beginning in 1932, to protest the theft of Ainu lands by the regional Japanese government. Using their own meagre funding, they lobbied any political leader who would listen. Failure of Peramonkoro's group to acquiesce to Japanese demands, even marginally, was not acceptable to the Japanese. The police constantly harassed them, often searching their hotel room and following the little group wherever they went, taking their pictures and labeling them "communists." In describing the event years later, Peramonkoro simply stated, "it was not a fun experience." In the end, the lobbying effort took longer than expected and so, when the group ran out of money, Peramonkoro and another woman made Ainu art and sold it to tourists throughout the Tokyo area.

This cultural confrontation created by Peramonkoro was the first time the Ainu were involved in a successful legal challenge of Japanese authority and, in 1934, the misappropriated "indigenous allowance land" was returned to the Ainu. It was during this period that Peramonkoro's leadership inspired a group of women to establish the Young Ainu Women's Association in an effort to fight discrimination against Ainu women, which was worse than the Ainu men experienced. While she burned with political fervor for equality, Peramonkoro also had to provide many of the families' income while the husbands tried to cultivate the woefully unproductive lands the Japanese 'gave' them. Using the basics of traditional design taught to her by her mother, she became one of the most respected textile artists in all of Ainu country. However, mastering the extremely complex abstractionism of Ainu wearable art did not produce enough income for family needs. Thus, demonstrating the same resolve she used in the land claim's dispute, she taught herself the intricacies of the art of creating the Japanese kimono and was a successful designer and fabric artist.

In addition to contributing to the families temporal needs, which also allowed her to satisfy her creative spirit, she became a much respected traditional performance artist. The Ainu have several areas of performance art, the most difficult being the singing of the *yukar*, which are songs of gods and of humans and rival the Greek odes in complexity and length. By design, the *yukar*, sung at major ceremonies such as the *iyomante*, the bear sending ceremony, never ends. It is said that Peramonkoro's lilting voice entranced the ceremony participants, who demanded that she continue singing hour after hour, long into the night. In later years, she and others tried to teach younger Ainu the beauty of the oral epics. However, the *yukar* is sung in the Ainu language and, as with most Native cultures, the traditional language was no longer the primary spoken language of the culture and, sadly, was almost lost.

Peramonkoro died in 1971 at the age of 74. I was 14 years old and if I knew of her passing, I do not remember it. To be honest, as a teenager, I did not want my world to be of the Ainu. I wanted, more than anything, to 'fit in' with the Japanese girl groups. The other children called me *dojin*, a pejorative term meaning Native in the Japanese language. Instead of celebrating the differences, I withdrew into a shell and stayed that way for the next 13 years. In 1984, I met, fell in love with, and married a mixed blooded Mohawk, Huron and French Canadian who was born in America. We moved to Washington state and I soon started attending Evergreen State College, where I wrote my first paper for a Native art history class on the fabric arts of Ainu women, because I knew little of the Native arts of the Northwest Coast at the time. It was then that I began to feel uncomfortable with my shallow knowledge of the art of my own people. The school had a large travel grant to research some aspect of a foreign culture and I applied with the intent to return to the home of my people and study Ainu textile art. Unbelievably, I received the grant. While happy that I was successful, I felt highly conflicted. Basically, I had walked away from the essence of my people and I felt guilty; I was not really sure what my interest was, and more importantly, who I was.

As I started my research in Hokkaido, I kept finding references to Peramonkoro the person, the activist and the artist. Ainu fabric art is completely abstract and when I saw some of Peramonkoro's traditional work, I noticed that it was more abstract and that the colour combinations were a little more exciting than the works of other women artists. In time, I was to discover that she influenced contemporary Ainu art more than any other person. Traditionally, the beautiful abstract designs were found solely on utilitarian objects such as wearable art, ceremonial art, and on some household items. Culturally speaking, art for the sole purpose of artistic expression was non-existent and, after a while, Peramonkoro found traditional Ainu artistic expectations very limiting and so began thinking 'out-of-the-box,' eventually challenging the status quo. She took Ainu signature designs to the next level of abstraction and developed a contemporary look by creating two-dimensional wall hangings, thereby influencing and encouraging a new generation of women artists to develop contemporary fine art textile traditions. While it may not seem a giant leap in the evolution of Ainu art, traditional cultural expectations had allowed only very little change in Ainu art over the previous 200 years.

The story behind Peramonkoro's influence on male gender art is most interesting. Bikky, the son she carried around Tokyo during the land protest lobbying effort, showed a remarkable talent for art at a very young age and so, breaking with tradition, Peramonkoro began to teach Bikky the design complexities of women's art. While this was embarrassing for Bikky at the time, by the time he was 20 years old, he was incorporating the designs into his woodcarvings. Before long, practically all Ainu carvers were experimenting with the 'new' look, which became known as *Bikky mon'yo* or, Bikky's patterns. While Bikky would often try to explain that he learned the patterns from his mother, the male dominated Japanese art world rarely acknowledged the contributions of this remarkable woman. There is not doubt that Peramonkoro's break from the tradition of gender-based art not only helped propel Bikky to international recognition, but also allowed gender crossing in the arts to become commonplace.

However, as I became more interested in Peramonkoro's art, I found myself more interested in Peramonkoro, the person. While I was especially interested in her courage, and impressed with her pride in her Ainu heritage, at the same time, I began to understand that a person's pride in their Native heritage is not a birthright, but must be earned. I found Peramonkoro's confrontation of discrimination and of cultural expectations very liberating. Even with life's challenges, she continued to exhibit a positive attitude throughout her life; for example, beginning in the late 1940s, she would spread blankets on the ground in the resort town of Akan and sell Ainu tourist art made by her husband. Tragically, her husband died in 1953, but she continued to move forward. She saved her money until she had enough to buy a small piece of land and eventually built an Ainu tourist shop, which is still operated by her youngest son. This modest Ainu business was the first to be owned by an Ainu woman.

It was at this time that she again displayed her strength of character. It was the custom in Akan that, several times a day, the Ainu would perform traditional dances for the tourists. Some Ainu criticized the practice believing it was 'selling' the Ainu culture, and accused the dancers of being 'tourist Ainu.' Peramonkoro often joined the dancers, and defended the performances, stating that to sing and dance the old songs with pride was to keep the culture alive. She felt strongly that entertainment was a legitimate form of education; if the Ainu did not educate others about Ainu culture, who would?

In 1964, she was asked to speak on the future of the Ainu at the Annual Ainu Culture Conference. She ended her speech with an emotional plea, "My fellow Ainu people, the pillars of the Ainu culture are the women. I ask you to educate our children and grandchildren about the enormous power of women so that they will grow up with pride about being born Ainu." In 1992, because of her leadership in preserving our culture, she was selected a legendary Ainu person thereby ensuring her legacy for those of us who need reminding that Native culture, in order to endure, most be nurtured. Peramonkoro, through her wisdom, showed us that, in order to survive, we must look within. To me, she will always be a guiding star in the Ainu sky.

••••

JOY HARJO

Joy Harjo is a poet, musician, writer and performer. She has published several books including her recently released: *How We Became Human, New and Selected Poems*. Other books of poetry include: *A Map to the Next World, Poems and Tales* and *The Woman Who Fell From the Sky*. Her first children's book is the *The Good Luck Cat* published by Harcourt. She has also co-edited an anthology of Native women's writing: *Reinventing the Enemy's Language, Native Women's Writing of North America*.

Joy is a saxophone player and performs nationally and internationally, solo and with a band. Her newest music project is a CD from Mekko Records: *Native Joy for Real*. She co-produced the award winning CD, *Letter From the End of the Twentieth Century* released by Silver Wave Records in 1997. Joy is a member of the Muscogee Nation, a member of the Tallahassee Wakokaye Grounds. She is a professor at UCLA and lives in Honolulu.

The Woman Who Fell from the Sky

Once a woman fell from the sky. The woman who fell from the sky was neither a murderer nor a saint. She was rather ordinary, though beautiful in her walk, like one who has experienced freedom from earth's gravity. When I see her, I think of an antelope grazing the alpine meadows in mountains whose names are as ancient as the sound that created the first world.

Saint Coincidence thought he recognized her as she began falling toward him from the sky in a slow spin, like the spiral of events marking an ascension of grace. There was something in the curve of her shoulder, a familiar slope that led him into the lightest moment of his life.

He could not bear it and turned to ask a woman in high heels for a quarter. She was of the family of myths who would give everything if asked. She looked like all the wives he'd lost. And he has nothing to lose anymore in this city of terrible paradox where a woman was falling toward him from the sky.

The strange beauty in heels disappeared from the path of Saint Coincidence, with all her money held tightly in her purse, into the glass of advertisements. Saint Coincidence shuffled back onto the ice to watch the woman falling and falling.

Saint Coincidence, who was not a saint, perhaps a murderer if you count the people he shot without knowing during the stint that took his mind in Vietnam or Cambodia – remembered the girl he yearned to love when they were kids at Indian boarding school.

He could still see her on the dusty playground, off in the distance, years to the west past the icy parking lot of the Safeway. She was a blurred vision of the bittersweet and this memory had forced him to live through the violence of fire.

There they stood witness together to strange acts of cruelty by strangers, as well as the surprise of rare kindness.

The woman who was to fall from the sky was the girl with skinned knees whose spirit knew how to climb to the stars. Once she told him the stars spoke a language akin to the plains of her home, a language like rocks.

He watched her once make the ascent, after a severe beating. No one could touch the soul masked by name, age and tribal affiliation. Myth was as real as a scalp being scraped for lice.

Lila also dreamed of a love not disturbed by the wreck of culture she was forced to attend. It sprang up here and there like miraculous flowers in the cracks of the collision. It was there she found Johnny, who didn't have a saint's name when he showed up for school. He understood the journey and didn't make fun of her for her peculiar ways, despite the risks.

Johnny was named Johnny by the priests because his Indian name was foreign to their European tongues. He named himself Saint Coincidence many years later after he lost himself in drink in a city he'd been sent to to learn a trade. Maybe you needed English to know how to pray in the city. He could speak a fractured English. His own language had become a baby language to him, made of the comforting voice of his grandmother as she taught him to be a human.

Johnny had been praying for years and had finally given up on a God who appeared to give up on him. Then one night as he tosses pennies on the sidewalk with his cousin and another lost traveler, he prayed to Coincidence and won. The event demanded a new name. He gave himself the name Saint Coincidence.

His ragged life gleamed with possibility until a ghost-priest brushed by him as he walked the sidewalk looking for a job to add to his stack of new luck. The priest appeared to look through to the boy in him. He despaired. He would always be a boy on his knees, the burden of shame rooting him.

Saint Coincidence went back to wandering without a home in the maze of asphalt. Asphalt could be a pathway to God, he reasoned, though he'd always imagined the road he took with his brothers when they raised sheep as children. Asphalt had led him here to the Safeway where a woman was falling from the sky.

The memory of all time relative to Lila and Johnny was seen by an abandoned cat washing herself next to the aluminum-can bin of the grocery store.

These humans set off strange phenomena, she thought and made no attachment to the thought. It was what it was, this event, shimmering there between the frozen parking lot of the store and the sky, something unusual and yet quite ordinary.

Like the sun falling fast in the west, this event carried particles of light through the trees.

Some say God is a murderer for letting children and saints slip through his or her hands. Some call God a father of saints or a mother of demons. Lila had seen God and could tell you God was neither male nor female and made of absolutely everything of beauty, of wordlessness.

This unnameable thing of beauty is what shapes a flock of birds who know exactly when to turn together in flight in the winds used to make words. Everyone turns together though we may not see each other stacked in the invisible dimensions.

This is what Lila saw, she told Johnny once. The sisters called it blasphemy.

Johnny ran away from boarding school for the first winter with his two brothers, who'd run away before. His brothers wrapped Johnny Boy, as they called him, with their bodies to keep him warm. They froze and became part of the stars.

Johnny didn't make it home either. The school officials took him back the next day. To mourn his brothers would be to admit an unspeakable pain, so he became an athlete who ran faster than any record ever made in the history of the school, faster than the tears.

Lila never forgot about Johnny, who left school to join the army, and a few years later as she walked home from her job at Dairy Queen she made a turn in the road.

Call it destiny or coincidence—but the urge to fly was as strong as the need to push when at the precipice of any birth. It was what led her into the story told before she'd grown ears to hear, as she turned from stone to fish to human in her mother's belly.

Once, the stars made their way down stairs of ice to the earth to find mates. Some of the women were angry at their inattentive husbands, bored, or frustrated with the cycle of living and dying. They ran off with the stars, as did a few who saw their chance for travel and enlightenment.

They weren't heard from for years, until one of the women returned. She dared to look back and fell. Fell through centuries, through the beauty of the night sky, made a hole in a rock near the place Lila's mother had been born. She took up where she had left off, with her children from the stars. She was remembered. This story was Lila's refuge those nights she'd prayed on her knees with the other children in the school dorms. It was too painful to miss her mother.

A year after she'd graduated and worked cleaning house during the day, and evenings, at the Dairy Queen, she laughed to think of herself wearing her uniform spotted with sweets and milk, as she left on the arms of one of the stars. Surely she could find love in a place that did not know the disturbance of death.

While Lila lived in the sky she gave birth to three children and they made her happy. Though she had lost conscious memory of the place before, a song climbed up her legs from far away, to the rooms of her heart.

Later she would tell Johnny it was the sound of destiny, which is similar to a prayer reaching out to claim her.

You can't ignore these things, she would tell him and it led her to the place her husband had warned her was too sacred for women.

She carried the twins in her arms as her daughter grabbed her skirt in her small fists. She looked into the forbidden place and leaped.

She fell and was still falling when Saint Coincidence caught her in his arms in front of the Safeway as he made a turn from borrowing spare change from strangers.

The children crawled safely from their mother. The cat stalked a bit of flying trash set into motion by the wave of falling—

or the converse wave of gathering together.

* * *

I traveled far above the earth for a different perspective. It is possible to travel this way without the complications of NASA. This beloved planet we call home was covered with an elastic web of light. I watched in awe as it shimmered, stretched, dimmed and shined, shaped by the collective effort of all life within it. Dissonance attracted more dissonance. Harmony attracted harmony. I saw revolutions, droughts, famines and the births of new nations. The most humble kindnesses made the brightest lights. Nothing was wasted.

I understood love to be the very gravity holding each leaf, each cell, this earthly star together.

• • • •

DEBRA ISABEL HURON

Debra Isabel Huron is a member of the Ontario Métis Aboriginal Association, a feminist, a wife, a mother, and a professional writer/editor. She was born in Sudbury, Ontario in 1953. Her family then moved to the tiny town of Missanabi (near Chapleau, Ontario) until it was time for her to begin grade one. In 1987, in honour of her Ojibwa great-grandmother who was from the Wikiwemikong Reserve on Manitoulin Island, Debra legally changed her surname to "Huron" The name Huron reflects Debra's love for the north shore of Lake Huron where the Georgian Bay surrounds the largest freshwater island in the world — the Manitoulin.

After graduating with a degree in Journalism in 1977 from Ryerson University in Toronto, Debra worked for newspapers in Fort Frances, Ontario and in Winnipeg. She moved to Ottawa in 1980 and was employed as media assistant to a New Democratic Party Member of Parliament on Parliament Hill. This was followed by jobs with Canada's largest labour union and with CUSO, where she spent six months in Botswana, Africa doing anti-apartheid work. Debra lived in Mexico, from 1990 to 1995. As a self-employed writer and editor, she now calls Ottawa home. With her husband and son, Debra makes frequent trips to Lake Temagami. The beauty of that part of Turtle Island continues to inspire her.

My aunt's kindness made a difference

"A cigarette, a cup of tea, and that'll do me."

With these words, my Aunt Nell would end a meal. Flipping back the heavy lid of a metal lighter and spinning the wheel that summoned fire, she would bend her head to light a MacDonald's menthol cigarette (thousands of them had stained her index and middle fingers yellow), before pouring herself a cup of Red Rose tea from a brown ceramic teapot.

Aunt Nell didn't own fancy china, or dainty things. She was a woman who kept her hair short and plain, a woman who never wore skirts or make-up, except for a swash of red lipstick on special occasions. Although she liked her beer, she never poured a glass when my sisters and I were visiting.

While Aunt Nell was enjoying her tea and her smoke, my sisters and I would be wolfing down pieces of her famous sour cream pie, a smooth, sweet confection filled with plump raisins. The sun would have set by this time, and the mood in her kitchen would be a bit sad because the end of supper meant we'd soon be going home after an afternoon of fun.

The winter Sunday afternoons we spent with Aunt Nell in the bungalow-without-a-basement that she rented on a laundry worker's wages became a regular part of my childhood when I was about 10 years old. Aunt Nell's influence on me was strongest for about two years – the years just before puberty, when I was still a girl.

What can we learn from another person's life? What lessons does an older woman with blood ties teach a girl? I don't have immediate answers to those questions. I only know that I would choose charcoal if I were to draw a portrait of my Aunt Nell, and I would make sure to blend soft shades of grey against the edges of the hard life she led.

When I was 10, my sister JoAnne was eight-and-a-half and our sister, Laura – who didn't always accompany us to Aunt Nell's house – was only seven, the baby in our family. During our afternoons with Aunt Nell, we played Cribbage, Rumoli, Rummy 500 and 21. Always covered with a plastic tablecloth, her steel-legged kitchen table was the site of an undeclared war between me and JoAnne. Both of us were more competitive than was proper for young girls in any historical period before or since. We were sure to snarl at each other whenever we lost. This meant that the end of every game was a potentially explosive time.

Aunt Nell curbed our baser instincts, not so much through what she said, because she didn't say a lot, and not by what she did because she wasn't someone given to grand gestures, or threats of physical punishment. The only rule she insisted on was that we must never cheat. And she somehow convinced us to look forward to the next game, the one that was waiting to be won. We came to believe that the loser this time might take the whole Rumoli pot the next time. She inspired this kind of hope.

I am now almost 50 years old, and my Aunt Nell has been dead for four years. She lived to be 84. When I look back on her life, I see hardship and even tragedy. But she never complained. Over the years, she drank more than her share of beer, when it was available. Maybe that was a silent complaint. Who can ever know what is deep in any person's heart? We can only know what is in our own hearts, and how we connect with those who open theirs to us.

Although Nell was my aunt, I think of her as my grandmother. And although she was my father's older sister, she was really the only mother he knew.

Aunt Nell had only one biological child, a daughter born in a home for unwed mothers, when Nell was only 19 years old. That child died in a car crash in 1952, the year before I was born. Maybe the loss of her daughter made Nell take the three of us – me and my two sisters – under her wing. But I don't think so. Nell just loved kids and she took care of lots of them during her lifetime.

Born in Port Caldwell, in what is now the District of Thunder Bay, Nell was the second daughter of a Métis man, James Pilon, and an American/Scotswoman, Eliza McCabe. Fishing was my grandfather's trade and he worked the waters around the Manitoulin Island almost all his life. On the Island, the family lived first at Meldrum Bay. Nell attended school two miles from the town, on the road to the lighthouse. She wrote and passed her grade eight exams. That was her education.

In 1930, life changed dramatically when my grandmother, Eliza, died at age 38, leaving seven children without a mother. The youngest in the family was three weeks old. My father was just a toddler. Nell was 16.

Settling in Providence Bay a year after their mother's death, the family lived in a long tarpaper and wood house next to the dock. Nell kept house for her father, brothers and sisters. She also cleaned Mrs. Ward's boarding house, for cash. But cash was always short, so the family survived the winters on whitefish netted from a nearby creek and on fry bread and potatoes – lots and lots of potatoes.

In 1933, taken advantage of by a local married man, Nell found herself pregnant. Her father sent her to a home for "wayward" girls at Sheguiandah. But a family in town got word to my great-grandmother, Mary Bemanakinang, who had been born on the Wikewemikong reserve but now lived in Killarney. This tiny woman (who smoked a pipe) heeded the call and made the journey from the mainland to urge her son to let Nell come home again. When the baby was born, Nell named her Daisy Ellen—a delicate name that didn't stick for long. The girl grew up with the nickname "Mick". After my grandfather's anger (or was it shame?) abated, Nell and her daughter moved back into the family home, where the blonde-haired Mick became a favourite – and a curiosity – among all her black-haired cousins.

Nell's daughter was 19 when she died in a car crash. It must have broken my aunt's heart to lose her beautiful daughter. She always kept a picture of the girl in her living room. It was a studio portrait, not a snapshot from somebody's Brownie camera, and it must have been taken just before Mick died, because the young woman with smooth blonde hair looked to be 17 or 18 years old. The frame that held the photo was as strong and solid as only a mother's love can be. I always felt a bit nervous seeing the photograph in its special place because Aunt Nell didn't talk about her dead daughter. Or about death. Death was a thief whose name would not be spoken.

Thirteen years after my grandmother died, my grandfather was felled by a heart attack. Nell left Manitoulin Island two years later to live in Sudbury. She never married. She always worked honest jobs for a living. For many years, she spent winters inside the steamy confines of a local dry cleaning firm. In the summer, she would muster as much vacation as possible so that she could fish with her common- law husband, a commercial fisher in Providence Bay. The only thing that ever put "free" money in her pocket was when this man died in 1964, leaving Nell his boat, his house and his commercial fishing license.

It was after his death that my sisters and I started to spend Sunday afternoons with Aunt Nell. I remember the big pot on her stove where a pig's head would boil, on its way to becoming headcheese. This "delicacy" was something Nell made as a special treat for my father. "When she would send it home with me, I would just hate even carrying the bag," my sister JoAnne remembers. It may be JoAnne's only bad memory of Aunt Nell.

To Aunt Nell, my sisters and I must have seemed like a modern, package deal: three girls with clean, shiny hair and fast tongues, girls whose future was sure to include comfort, money and good health. She didn't always have the first two things, at least in her early years, but Aunt Nell taught me that there was really nothing in life to complain about. She always had good health, and she believed there was much in life to be grateful for.

Any girl who has a kind, older woman as part of her life is a lucky girl. And Aunt Nell was "older" the whole time I knew her. She was about 50 when we started going to her house to play cards, and as I grew older, I was always happy to visit her at Christmas. It was good to know she was still walking to her job every day, rain or shine. She never owned a car, or even got a driver's licence, and she spent her whole life on Manitoulin Island and in Sudbury. When I was in my 30s and told her about the places I had lived – Africa and Mexico – she always shook her head in a kind of disbelief. "I don't know," she would say. I didn't try to figure out exactly what this meant, I just accepted that the kind of life I had was something that she could not easily understand.

Books took Aunt Nell to places she would not otherwise go. With only a grade eight education, she was an avid reader. She always had a paperback novel on the go. Sometimes, I would see the books she hoped to read stacked in a pile on the end-tables in her living room. Other times, when I went into her bedroom to fetch a chair or to let the cat in through that room's only window, I would see a thick novel perched on her bedside table. Aunt Nell liked romance novels and cowboy stories. The fact that she enjoyed reading encouraged me to read, too.

When she was in her 70s, retired from her job as floor walker in the dry cleaning firm, and living in a basement apartment at her sister's home in Sudbury, my Aunt Nell was still smiling and always pleasant when visitors came. "If I met you on the street," she told me, a few years before she died, "I wouldn't know you." Alzheimer's was eating away at Aunt Nell's brain. She almost giggled when she admitted that her own niece was a stranger to her.

The last time I saw her, she was in a government nursing home. When I walked down the hall to find a washroom, I couldn't help noticing a big sign on the fire exit door: "Nellie, do not open the door." She had been trying to escape! I admired her spunk at the same time that I realized it was Alzheimer's that made her want to wander.

"A cigarette, a cup of tea, and that'll do me." With these homey words, my Aunt Nell broadcast contentment. I honour that contentment, that ability to accept the cards that she was dealt, and to play those cards in a winning game.

My Aunt Nell gave me what I most needed in those years before I became a teenager. She gave me kindness and the time to play games. As I grow older, moving from womanhood back to a kind of girlhood, I know there is wisdom in what she taught me, and I try to find ways to make room in my life for kindness, and the time to play games.

In the end, it seems to me, these two simple things are what make any life worth living.

(The author would like to thank the brother and sister team of Adelaide Campbell and Joe Pilon for providing details of the family history.)

••••

LEE MARACLE

Lee Maracle was born in North Vancouver, British Columbia, and is a member of the Sto:loh nation. She is the mother of four and grandmother of four. Lee is an award-winning author and her works include, *Bobbi Lee, Ravensong, Sundogs* (novels), *I Am Woman* (non-fiction), *Bent Box* (poetry) and *Sojourner's Truth* (short story collection). She has co-edited a number of works including, *My Home As I Remember*, and *Women and Language Across Cultures*. Her new novels, *Daughters Are Forever* and *Will's Garden* received positive reviews by both *The Globe and Mail* and at the Returning the Gift Conference of Native Writers. Lee is also a teacher and was a Distinguished Visiting Professor of Canadian Culture at Western Washington University in Bellingham, USA.

Sometimes I cannot locate myself anywhere. I believe I am here, in any city, anywhere on Turtle Island, in this particular century, which also happens to be a different millennium from the one in which I was born, but then I run smack dab into a conundrum that gets me wondering in what century I am in. It is dislocating to be dislodged from the time frame of your fellow citizens. I feel dislodged and so am dislocated. When I feel that way, I return to origin.

Sometime back, I received a call for submission from Native Women in the Arts and decided that I would wrestle with my arrogance, even what little humility I have, my knowledge and myself and write a response. In fact, I was determined to fight like hell with whatever - until I came up with an article for submission. As a writer, I am invariably asked, "Who are your influences?" As an imagined Native "leader" I am asked, "Who are your role models and heroes?" People toss these two questions in my direction about twice annually at the very least, twice monthly during a new book release year. I released two books this year, so I feel peppered with them. I am always embarrassed to answer. As a writer, my greatest influence was *The Oxford English Dictionary* – all 13 volumes. Whole stories came out of word chases and games I played with the Oxford boys, (my volumes are old, so no girls helped defining the words). As a Native, I am pretty much expected to have a 'role model or a hero', or else how did I 'make it'? If I can't think of a role model or a hero, the acrid taste of arrogance begins to threaten the back of my throat.

I look up the words in my dictionary. I know that is petty, but petty is what makes me a good writer. A role model is "a person looked to by others as an example (model) in a particular role or situation". There it is: the conundrum: "Native women role models", so is it the "woman" part that is the role and the Native part the situation? Or is it vice versa. I can't for the life of me decide. I suddenly realize that this business of "role model" doesn't really exist for white people in quite the same way. White people are called upon to look up to professionals: police officers, fireman, teachers, mentors etc., but when the government handed that part of their culture to us, they handed it over as though we had no real professions, just situations, roles to be played, not people with roles in different situations. I decline to define any Native woman as a role or a situation, but the underlying desire for this book, our need of it, continues to call me.

Heroic and influence are both options. I begin with heroic. Behind me the trail is littered with dead women relatives – more than a 100 in my lifetime and we number only a few hundred souls today, so about one sixth of my women didn't make it as far as I have in life. Many of them killed themselves. That makes all those who did survive heroic – all of us – me too. Of the dead, at least 30 lived heroically – that is about one third of them. I reach beyond family. I interacted with my Native women pretty steadily most of my life so there must be someone out there I can write about. I look at my address index – I know a little over 5,000 people. Most of them are women. One of them will surely stand out more than the others. I begin to realize that every woman that I have befriended has also interacted with her community.

Most of the people who created our modern organizations – which number now in the thousands – were women. None of them were paid to do this, so they worked at day jobs and volunteered after work. Most of them had children. There was no money to begin the arduous building, so they sacrificed time, raised money for their goals. Stories flood back…"We had bake sales, made cookies and cakes and sold them to each other." I laugh. A nostalgic and appreciative tear drops. A dozen or so stalwart women, occasionally assisted by a man, built each of the hundreds of organizations that perform a multitude of services in our world from treatment centres to legal aid. There are in my home province about 10,000 Native women holding up the sky right now. Many of them are on my address list. I know them. The majority, 50 per cent of the 100,000 Natives in British Columbia are children, and half the adult population are men. That means of the 25,000 adult Native women, 10,000 of them volunteer or work in these organizations. Canada wide, that number swells, threatens to spin out of control. The majority of these women grew up poor, under educated, and struggled with their schooling, mothered children, built organizations and served the community while reclaiming culture, doing healing work on themselves and others. Most did so as single moms. They are all heroic.

Even if I narrow the numbers of women to those extremely knowledgeable and brilliant women I know, the number is still staggering. The 3,000 or so Native women I know were among the 150 women who launched the Friendship Centre movement in the 1950s when white people were busy hating the hell out of us. They were determined to end race hatred in this country. It is on the way out the door because of the heroism of these mothers of bridge building, friendship and peace. Among the 3,000 women I know, are about 100 women students who launched the Native Student Unions across the country at a time when we weren't allowed to have "separate or independent organizations" on the grounds that it was 'reverse racism'. Among the 3,000 women I know are 200 or so young women and kids who closed the first residential school in 1968 and withstood the attack of the church, the state, the media, the police and even some of our parents - and won. Among the 3,000 women I know, are about 350 women who were the first to disclose residential school abuse, all of whom stuck to their guns under threat of death and excommunication from the church. As a result of their courage, some of them suffered exile from their communities. Among the 3,000 women I know, are several hundred who faced gun-toting, baton-wielding police and vigilantes who tried to stop them from eating every time they went out to exercise their right to fish. The ink that penned the laws stopping them from eating is fading because these women kept on fighting until they won. Among the 3,000 women I know, are all kinds of women who went to school, raised a family, battled racist landlords, stereotypes, teachers, etc. and got through. Among the 3,000 women I know, are 13 old women, who offered to get arrested on behalf of the old growth timber (cedar trees) of Lyle Island, who inspired a whole nation to rise off its knees fight for its homeland - its legacy, and won. Among the 3,000 women I know, are hundreds who mothered children and fought urban epidemics such as AIDS, hepatitis and malnutrition. All of these women headed their communities and their nations in the direction of social transformation, sovereignty, national and gender improvement and succeeded.

My mother and a dozen other women took on the state and Native organizations and fought for Indigenous control of Indigenous childcare and won. I took on the publishing industry and won. My sister...my aunts...my grandma...my friends... all have taken on some battle and won. They aren't my role models because I did not pick up any of those battles. These women definitely influenced and inspired me, earning my gratitude and respect. My problem is not that I don't have any heroes, nor am I short of women who have influenced me. My problem is that there are just too many Native heroines in my life.

I have thought about this for six months now. "One of the many heroic women in my life must stand out more than the others," I insist to myself. How shall I pick her? Should I pick the most famous, so everyone can recognize her? – Without a doubt, that would be Maria Campbell or Jeannette C. Armstrong, both of whom carry the responsibility of being authors, filmmakers, international political and environmental activists, speakers, directors, businesswomen, language speakers, teachers, grandmothers, mothers, wives, sisters, and friends to me and 1000 others. They are path cutters, institution builders and influential beyond the reasonable. But then Alanis Obomsawin pops up, award-winning political documentary film producer, poet, women's rights advocate, mother, grandmother, and sovereignty activist. After that, Nilak Butler comes into view, actress, environmental and, women's rights activist, singer, speaker, poet and intellectual. Marcia Gomez follows. Then Dr. Donna Goodleaf. Then Dorothy Christian, Gerry Ambers, Ceis

Wies, Columpa C. Bobb, Jeanne Carter, Amy George, Sandra Laronde, Carol Greyeyes, my ta'ah...my aunts...the women come rushing at me so fast I can't slow them down to see who they are. I see all these women coming over this hill in their hundreds, in their thousands, all smiling, some wearing jaunty flowered scarves, others old straw hats, some in dramatic black and red blankets, others with intricately beaded jackets, some in suits, some in torn jeans...some armed with cameras, others with briefcases, others with pens, paint brushes, some have needles and thread, others pad and paper; some are young, some are old and some are in between, but they all deserve my accolades.

Some come over the hill dancing, others cooking, others playing with children, some pump gas, others sell raffle tickets or take care of the children of the women who are on picket lines, boycotting or leafleting teaching or building some organization or other. Some choreographed their own dances, others danced to the choreography of others, and some wrote the words they performed, some performed the words others wrote, some managed the performers, and others publicized the performance. Some held boom mikes, others stood at podiums, others grew medicine flowers, and some healed the sick. Some of these women fought for our future, some fought for our present and some fought for our past. There they were, every single woman I knew, rushing at me, each one deserving their moment in the sun. I am tempted to struggle to list them.

I begin to get discouraged. I start to rationalize, well hell, white people heroize each other, that's not our way. What are we doing singling someone out as better than all the rest for anyway? I chastise myself and say, "quit rationalizing, let the women come; maybe I will just have to name them all." The truth is that every Native woman who has ever held a job, raised a child, launched an organization is a hero worthy of emulating. We need to acknowledge our heroic women, I need to acknowledge the heroic women in my life – but in truth about 25 per cent of the women in Indian country are heroic and very influential and I have been blessed to meet thousands of them.

I am about to throw in the towel, when the line opens up and behind the women is this little clutch of three tiny girls; they cannot be more than four or five years old. I see them skip to the front. As they come closer, I recognize them. I begin to weep with particular pride and joy. These are my heroes, the ones who most influenced me, and the ones who I wish to give you for this auspicious and desperately needed publication:

Lee-Lee

It was 1952; Lee-Lee sat on an old stovetop and watched people come in and out of her life. The stovetop was never lit; her mom could never seem to come up with the cash to fill the stove with oil. It sat there and Lee-Lee used it to watch the world. She studied the human beings as they partied, staggered about drunk, worked, played, sang or danced or talked about the community, its needs, and white people with their hatred and the world and its injustice. She tried so hard to figure out why they did the things they did. She never figured that out, but she taught me a thing or two: keep your mind curious, study people, they will always surprise and teach you something. Just when you least expect it, they will drop some little pearl of wisdom in your path. Collect and braid the imagined threads of their character slowly and with loving care; you never know which human you will come to love.

Lumpy

Lumpy always loved going to the theatre even when she was a little child. She had this adorable Little Red Riding Hood-style coat that was waterproof and went from tip to toe. She had it in her arms one morning.
"Mommy, let's go to da featre."
"I have no money," I answered.
"Da Featre in da park is free," she reminds.
"It costs money to take the bus."
"I have a coat and boots. We could walk."
"It's a long way." I am losing this argument and already planning how to achieve the end. I mentally map out the difficulties and figure out how to overcome each one.

"I am strong," she says, puffing out her little chest and doing a west coast squat – one of our basic dance moves. I give in. We pack up a lunch and head to the park – seven miles– this four-year-old put one foot in front of the other and never once complained. I could see the strain on her, but I could also see her wilfullness, her beautiful determination, her self-reliance and her absolute love for *Shakespeare In the Park*. Lumpy taught me never to give up on cultural life. If we are going to knock ourselves out, overwork and push the envelope then let art and cultural joy be the end.

Tin-Tin

We have just finished watching *Shakespeare in the Park*. Lumpy straggles behind; I am pregnant and so cannot carry her the last half kilometre. Pretty soon, I hear this little voice squeezing out "Wait…Mom", between heavy grunts. I turn. Tania, who is actually smaller then her younger sister, is piggybacking Lumpy whose legs are now very sore. I suck wind and sigh. I am so angry at the level of heroism required by Native kids to have an ordinary life, rich in culture and being. I wait for her to catch up. As soon as Tin-Tin looks up, she smiles. Tin-Tin taught me to push hard only for the things and people you love so that you can smile and keep on pushing.

Kwani & Niimke

Two little girls blow bubbles in the air; dancing and circling to some inaudible music that plays inside their bodies. They laugh. I watch for a while. The dance changes, for a moment each is lost in their own music and dance, they twirl, see each other and then for a moment they dance together, then go off on their own again. As they recognize each other, their giggles gain volume and significance, off on their own, there is a look of bliss that is sweet and private. From these two little gals, I learned the joy of weaving in and out of collaboration and returning to our individual choreography in this great dance called life.

Each one of the heroic women who influenced me was once a child, like the ones above that I know so well: my daughters, my granddaughters and myself. Each woman must have been a little girl like me who sat on some stovetop, tabletop, rock or cliff or lake edge and wondered about others, about the world, or danced like my little granddaughters, alone and together, or sucked wind, puffed up their chest, gritted their teeth as did my daughters, and pushed for what they loved. Heroism begins with the child. The little girl who sticks out her little chest and just refuses to take no for an answer, she is my little hero. Or the little girl who choreographs her own dance, then slips into collaborating with the dance of another girl with joy and alacrity, these are the women who influence me.

I can picture Sandra Laronde, sitting on the stones of Lake Temagami and wondering about the world of women, setting herself up for heroism later in life.

••••

BIRDY MARKERT

Birdy Markert is a Witsuwit'en wife and mother of two children named Brandon and Alannah. Her clan membership falls under the House of Many Eyes from the Likhsilyu clan. She has been a teacher in the Bulkley Valley School District for the past six years and she is the newly appointed District Aboriginal Principal for her district and her people.

Her grandmother, Josephine Michell, who is now 96 years old, raised her on a reserve in Northern British Columbia. Birdy was raised doing and learning all the same activities her grandmother, Josephine, learned from her mother, Amelia: catching salmon, setting traps, hunting, preparing traditional foods, and so much more. Although Birdy has had a good teacher, she cannot fluently speak her Native language, but can understand it fluently.

Birdy has completed a Bachelor of Education degree at the University of British Columbia, with a double major in First Nations Education and Language Arts and also is a spokesperson for her people's children and families.

My Grandmother, My Hero

My grandmother was born February 20, 1909 in a cabin with no running water at a place called Beamont, which was a Canadian National Railway Whistle Stop between Moricetown and Hazelton, British Columbia. Although she never received any formal education and does not read or write, she is the smartest woman I know. She has seen the world change so much over the past 93 years that I sometimes wonder what she thinks of the way we live today.

In her time, she lived entirely off of the land because they did not have grocery stores to buy food. Everything her family ate, they harvested directly from the land. Her mother, Amelia, taught her to cook over an open fire to help out while her family spent their time working out on the land.

When my grandmother taught me to cook, it was on an electric stove. I did not pack wood to keep the stove hot like she did. My grandmother learned how to make medicines from the earth; I buy medicines from the pharmacy. My grandmother learned how to make buckskin out of moose hide and to use it to make clothes and blankets; I buy my clothes and blankets from the store. My grandmother trapped animals for their furs to keep herself warm and to sell to the Hudson's Bay Co.; I trapped furs as a child, but as an adult, I buy my furs for decoration from the store. My grandmother learned to fish with gaffs, weirs, and later gill nets; she taught me to fish with a gill net, but today I order my fish from Wet'suwet'en Fisheries. My grandmother would walk 37 kilometers to visit her cousins in Hazelton; when I visit my cousins in Hazelton, I drive there.

My grandmother is the matriarch of our family. She keeps our stories strong and our songs sung. She directs us during feasts. She keeps the peace and gently reminds us to respect and love each other and to be patient with each other. She loves us despite our faults. I admire her for raising a large extended family, running a logging camp, teaching us about our environment, and accepting all of us as her children.

She taught us the value of hard work. She taught us how to keep food on the table. She taught us how to harvest and preserve what our territory provides. She taught us to be kind and firm. She is the reason I am who I am today. She is my grandmother. She is Josephine Michell and she is my hero.

••••

MARIJO MOORE

MariJo is of Cherokee, Irish, and Dutch descent. She is an author, artist, essayist, editor, and publisher. Her publications include: *The Diamond Doorknob, Spirit Voices of Bones, Red Woman With Backward Eyes and Other Stories, Crow Quotes, Tree Quotes, The Cherokee Little People,* and *The First Fire;* she is also the editor of *Genocide of the Mind: New Native Writing.* MariJo resides in the mountains of western North Carolina.

Remembering Beloved Woman Maggie Wachacha

Some of the strongest women I admire are Cherokee women: strong in intuition, determination, and tradition. Not always acknowledged for their contributions, many Cherokee women are left standing in the shadows of male leaders. I often speculate how hard life must have been for women during the Removal Era. When I gave birth to my son, I was in a hospital where my needs and his could be met. What if I had given birth on a quilt laid out in the woods, or even on the bare ground while walking hundreds of miles to an unknown land? Would I have survived? Would he? Many didn't. I believe more acknowledgements should be given to the contributions of our female ancestors and what they have had to endure.

When the Europeans first came to this land and began "investigating" the ways of the Cherokee, they were appalled at what they referred to as a "petticoat government." The Cherokee had a Women's Council, the head of which was the Beloved Woman, whom they believed the Creator spoke through. The Cherokee held their women in high regard. By tribal law, the penalty for killing a woman was double that for killing a man because of the children she might have borne.

A Beloved Woman is one who is extremely influential in tribal affairs: a woman who speaks in council meetings and communicates with Beloved Women of other nations. In years past, a Beloved Woman was sometimes known as War Woman because she had the power of life and death over captives of war. She also had a voice in deciding whether or not the nation would go to war.

In 1984, the joint councils of the Eastern Band of Cherokees and the Cherokee Nation of Oklahoma conferred the title of Beloved Woman on Maggie Ax Wachacha, a traditionalist from Robbinsville on Qualla Boundary. For over 40 years, Maggie was the clerk for the Tribal Council, transcribing all proceedings into the Cherokee language for official records. She walked 60 miles from her home in the Snowbird Township in Robbinsville to the council house in downtown Cherokee, never missing a meeting. When she and her husband, Jarrett Wachacha, who also sat on Tribal Council, had enough money, they would take the train. They left at midnight in order to arrive in Cherokee the next day in time for a meeting.

According to a family member, Maggie was born in 1895, in the Little Snowbird Township to Wil and Caroline Cornsilk Ax. She married her husband, who was of the Deer (Awi) Clan in 1935. Maggie was from the Wolf (Waya) Clan. This clan membership was passed on to her daughters, Winona and Lucinda, as is customary in a matrilineal society.

Maggie was also well known as a traditional Indian doctor. Taught by her grandmother the natural ways of medicine, she traveled many miles to attend to the needs of others. Maggie assumed various responsible and demanding roles in her long life. She was a magnificently strong woman who worked hard for the survival of her people.

••••

RICHIE PLASS

Richie Plass lives in Green Bay, Wisconsin and is of Menominee and Stockbridge-Munsee descent. He is an entertainer, who plays the drums with a country music group, and a lecturer. Richie's lectures cover topics such as education, culture, traditions, professional environment and social impact. In addition, he has held sessions on Menominee and general Native American issues, including culture, history, lore, performing arts, traditions, and cross-cultural relations.

Richie has an Associate Degree in Architecture, is the Director of Tribal Economic Development on the Menominee Reservation, is involved in diversity training, and is the sports editor for his school paper. Richie is also a published poet. In the spring of 1999, he spent three months as a citizen member of the Press-Gazette Editorial Board.

Ingrid Washinawatok El-Issa

In March of 1999, along with two of her companions, my cousin Ingrid Washinawatok El-Issa was murdered in Bolivia, South America. She and her companions were there to assist the Uwa tribe with the advancement of their tribal educational programs; however, members of the Revolutionary Armed Forces of Colombia decided that, by killing these three Americans, their movement would draw more recognition to their cause. The three Americans were not delegates or representatives of the United States government; rather, they were educators, visiting Bolivia to assist an Indigenous people in educating their children and other tribal members. What happened after the murders demonstrates the excessive injustice subjected upon Native Americans by the federal government.

After days of not knowing and getting the run around from the Justice Department, word was finally sent to our family on the reservation that, not only had these three activists been kidnapped, they had been murdered. To add insult to injury, our family was not permitted to, or given any assistance in, getting her body home. Thus, after a few months, I wrote an editorial entitled, "Once again, death brings injustice to Indian Nation," and since that time, my words proved to be very prophetic.

John Kennedy, Jr.'s plane went down off Martha's Vineyard. President Clinton literally brought out the whole armed forces to assist in the search for the wreckage and passengers. Now, I am not saying John Kennedy Jr. did not deserve this attention and assistance, but our family continuously called the White House, the Justice Department and other federal agencies, and was not assisted in any way.

Shame on America! Once again, it was apparent that fame and money speak louder than anything.

When Ingrid's body was finally brought home and we sent her on her journey, our family could rest. To pay respects to Ingrid at her funeral, there were two Nobel Peace Prize winners in attendance along with representation from, not only Indian tribes throughout the United States, but also from people from around the world.

As I have continued my writing, speeches, presentations and performances, I have had the honour of meeting many people who Ingrid touched in one way or another. One of the most enlightening experiences was at the "Indian Summer Fest" in Milwaukee in September of 2001, where my band was performing. On the same stage as my band, was a group from Long Island, New York called, "The Thunderbird Sisters." They won a Native American Music Award in recent years and I was honored to have the opportunity to introduce them as they took the stage for their performance. However, it wasn't until Sunday that we realized our connection.

All of Sunday's performances were cancelled that year because of a huge rainstorm and, while standing around backstage and telling stories, as I am accustomed to doing, the members of The Thunderbird Sisters found out I was Ingrid's cousin. We spent the next hour or so sharing stories and getting to know each other on a special level. I told them of my writing and things I was doing to keep Ingrid's life work alive, so they asked me to send them some of my poetry. I actually went one step further and wrote a special poem, *Carrying A Message Far From Home*, just for them. I wanted them to know the honour I felt in getting to know them, how much I had enjoyed their performances and that I wanted to somehow tie it all together with one piece.

Recently, the members of The Thunderbird Sisters have returned the favour: I received a phone call from them this past winter, at which time they told me that they put music to the poem I wrote for them, are performing it on stage, and would like for me to come to New York to play the drumming tracks for the proposed recorded album version; I am truly honoured and I know Ingrid would be too.

••••

JANET MARIE ROGERS

Janet Marie Rogers is a visual artist, writer and playwright of Mohawk/Tuscarora ancestry from the Six Nations Territory in southern Ontario. Janet has seven self-published chapbooks of poetry and two books of poems published by Fine Words Chapbooks in Victoria, British Columbia, where Janet has been a resident since 1994.

Janet enjoys giving public readings of her work in the many cities she travels to, such as the National Museum of the American Indian in New York City and in the Hirshorn Museum in Washinton, D.C. Janet has incorporated movement into her readings, which are expressed as spoken word performances. Her artwork graces the pages of her book, *Mixed Meditations (of an Urban Indian)*, and her photographs are included in her latest book, *Sun Dance, Poems from the Red Road*. In the summer of 2000, while at the Gibralter Point Centre of the Arts on Toronto Island, Ontario, Janet created a play featuring Mohawk poetess, E. Pauline Johnson, and legendary painter, Emily Carr. In addition, her short stories are part of national anthologies.

Sky Woman

Sky Woman: she is my personal hero, icon, source of inspiration and guiding light – my almighty motivator, mother, and sister in the struggle. What I know of her may not be consistent or accurate as a result of the faulty written work, translations and artistic license. However, Sky Woman is more than fiction, legend and myth; she is real. In fact, I see her everyday, everywhere in the faces and acts of courage and through every red woman on the street. Be they busy suit wearing, ambitious tight-haired, pursed-lipped, fast-paced, urban-go-getters or single moms, buggy-pushing, welfare dependent caught in the city struggle, searching for a way out survivalist, Sky Woman is part of us all. She left bits of herself in our grandmothers, our faceless, nameless female ancestors right on down the line. You and I carry her in our blood and bones, our hair and skin today.

Sky Woman came from the stars. She fell like an angel to what was not yet earth. She was here even before the drum was born, or did she bring the drum within her, inside her big pregnant belly? Sky Woman is both the stardust we entrust our prayers with and the magic from which we spin our own spells. She is the first woman, numero-uno, the ultimate pioneer; she must have had her sun in Aries and her moon in Aquarius to take on a position like that. Sky Woman may have been exhibiting profound clumsiness in her tumble through the hole in the sky world, or performing an act of brilliant cunning in an attempt to escape an overbearing chief/husband who denied her, her maternal cravings. I think her accidental escape is the very thing we humans can attribute our existence to today.

Perfect accidents of significance, perfect acts that created endless ripples of more perfect acts living out the universal perfect plan, accident after accident after accident, all perfectly planned.

She, our original Mother Earth – Sky Woman: understanding of animal talk and earth communications. She embodies human good and human evil, literally, with twin sons who possess both traits. She taught us, through example, that to expel both elements, to rid one's system completely of both good and evil, means a certain death. As she purged her sons into the perfect world, she released balance into the universe. Sky Woman died in the birth process. She was killed by her sons' struggle within her to break free of each other; they live as night and day, light and dark, positive and negative. She is the grand teacher; we learn so much from the example of her brief and peril filled life. We learn the importance of letting go – we can fall in humility, with trust, through our own personal portals just as Sky Woman did, falling, dropping, plummeting to worlds yet unborn. Sky Woman rejected the conventional life of wife and chose instead to break brand new ground. She is the original astronaut, astral traveler existing in one dimension as easily as another.

I admire, adore and wholeheartedly receive the teachings Sky Woman left in her wake. Her strength and spirit, her female beauty, in all her pregnant glory, her selfless sacrifices and her bravery – the same bravery that speaks to red women spirits and encourages us to get up, get out, be seen, be heard, and never be silenced on or off reserve, in or out of employment, with or without our children, connected or disconnected to family. She has generously blessed our Nations of the East, South, West, and North and provided us with a continental playground to live, and learn, love and carry on.

••••

MARLENE ROGERS

Marlene Rogers was born in Hamilton, Ontario where she currently resides with her husband of 49 years. Her career, other than that of wife and mother of three children, has been in the secretarial field. She began working on a part time basis at the age of 15 and, after high school graduation, continued full time until the birth of her first child. From then on, most of her employment continued part time because of her growing family. Her last place of employment was a full time position at McMaster University, where she was secretary to the Chairman of Continuing Education until her retirement in 1996.

In 1999, retirees of McMaster University were invited to submit inter-generational stories. She chose as her subject, her granddaughter, Ashley. Of the four stories she submitted, two were chosen to appear in *Exchanges Between Us*, the McMaster University publication.

My Hero
My Aunt – (Cora) Eva Baptiste

Heroes come in many different sizes, shapes and colours. Most heroes are thought of as having performed daring physical feats. The Webster Dictionary describes a hero as "a man admired for his achievements and qualities." That pretty well sums up my hero; although there was no pomp and pageantry with bands playing and flags waving, no ticker tape parade, even no overt act of heroism at all. Her heroism was not a response action to a single deed. Her heroism was in the way she lived her life; although not as a saint, mind you. I'm sure she had her trips and stumbles along the way, as did many renowned heroes. So let me introduce you to my hero as I put memories to paper to paint that picture for you.

My hero, who has cloaked me in such wonderful memories, is my Aunt Eva – my mother's sister. You might ask then, why not my mother? Don't think, not for one minute, that the wonderful memories of my mother are not there – they most definitely are, but for all too short of a time. My mother died when I was 13. At 13, I thought nothing in the world could ever fill the void left by her death, and it wasn't until I was old enough to visit on my own that I came to know another hero – her sister – my Aunt Eva.

I know very little of her early life, but I'm sure that her philosophy of how to live life must have been formed then. Native records indicate that my Aunt (Cora) Eva Garlow was born on October 19, 1898 and, although baptized as such, she was always known as Eva. She married John Baptise (born March 26, 1887) on November 5, 1916. Both were Lower Mohawk members of the Six Nations

Reservation of Hagersville, Ontario. They eventually settled into married life in a modest home – no frills, just the essentials. If ever they had a quarrel, as I'm sure they must have, it was kept private, as never was there any evidence of lingering friction between them.

While assisting my uncle John to secure the barn during a severe storm, the top half of the double barn door was blown off, striking and breaking my aunt's hip. Her hip was improperly set, which left her with a limp that eventually required the use of a cane – but what she learned to do with that cane. No complaints, to my knowledge, were ever heard regarding her disability. "Disability!", she would say, "Things happen, and you just have to make the best of it." What a credo that sustained her many times throughout her life. She just tackled that adversity like she did so many things. She turned the negative to a positive, and as she said, "got on with things." Tins and jars of preserves on the top shelves were never inaccessible to my aunt – just using the crook of her cane, down they would come. We used to tell her that she could be a catcher for any baseball team. Many years later, my feisty aunt used that same cane late one evening when she responded to a knock on her door. I'm sure that drunken man thought twice before ever knocking on her door again.

My uncle John made the cane by wrapping one end of a stout twig around a tree to form the handle. Living with the cane became normal for her: lift this, push that there, and pull this over here. I am now the possessor of that cane and am not sure if it is time, medicine or the spirit of that cane that sees me through bouts of occasional back pain.

When my uncle passed away in November of 1972, I asked her if she was finding it difficult to live alone and she answered, "It's not easy to live alone, but you just have to get on with your life and do what's needing doing, one day at a time. You do the best that you can."

Coal oil lamps and wood stoves were often causes of fires. When the news of these disasters was heard, Aunt Eva was among the first to pack up of her homemade quilts, bring some of those top shelved items down with her cane, tuck a few hard-earned dollars into a box, and deliver her care package to the victims. Uncle John, too, would be among the men helping to do restorations.

I remember visiting my aunt with my mother one summer, when I was eight. My aunt never had any children, and neighbourhood children were miles away, so I didn't have any playmates. One afternoon was set aside for my mother to be part of a quilting bee. The quilting frame, which was made by my uncle, was set up in the big kitchen and surrounded by chairs seating eight giggling women. With nothing to do, I crawled underneath the quilt-in-progress and watched eight needles wave in and out of the partly assembled quilt, while the eight ladies 'tee-heed' all afternoon. Later in life, I contributed to my aunt's quilts; what satisfaction it was to see scraps of material from my sewing, or a piece from a good part of one of my husband's worn-out shirts, or some of the material dropped off by friends and neighbours. I still have some of these treasured quilts. A panorama of cherished memories floods out when I bring different ones out to change my décor for the season. The pink one for summer, the one with the most orange in it for fall and, of course, the red-backed ones for Christmas. Even now, just walking through fabric stores and seeing the country prints takes me immediately back to that wonderful big warm kitchen and those long-gone, 'tee-heeing' women. Today, my granddaughter enjoys playing with the jars of buttons that my aunt always saved long before the term recycle was ever used.

Every Sunday possible found my aunt in church, where she taught a Sunday school class. Before leaving home, the wood stove would be lit for, perhaps, a roast or piece of mouthwatering brisket that would be part of the evening meal; her hat would be set atop her head, just so, and her dress smoothed down; and away she would go. You don't often hear the word 'tithe' anymore, but tithe my aunt did from their meagre funds. For church socials, it was a foregone conclusion that pies would be forthcoming from my aunt. Although it is difficult for me to paint the picture with words to describe my hero, it is almost equally as difficult to find the words to described her pies and baking. The apple pie was the best – no, elderberry – maybe pumpkin. Oh my gosh, not to mention the lemon, preserved raspberry, strawberry, cherry, black cap, raisin, and mincemeat! The pies were always my aunt's domain.

My aunt kept a scrapbook and, one of the articles that she cut out from a newspaper, reads as follows:

Dear God

May You grant us the promise of to-morrow,
wisdom so softly we may tread
patience to seek out the truth,
gratitude for counties wide spread.

May You grant us faith in the future,
love for our fellow-men too,
a keener concern for out nations' welfare,
determination to see things thru.

May You give us words when we need them
to comfort the sick and the sad,
to encourage to-day's youth to hold on, to say
thank you to the kind neighbours we've had.

May You give us the strength to withstand
the evils that we face to-day,
to think of the need of others,
And be mindful of them when we pray.

As her health was failing, my aunt had to come to terms with entering a nursing home. At first, she was confined to the Lady Wellington nursing home during the winter months only and returned home in the spring. With a little assistance from family and neighbours, she was able to live this way for a few years. Finally, the day came when she knew, deep in her heart, that she would not be returning home in the spring; the only tears shed were mine, not hers. Again, her credo, "you just have to do the best you can," sustained her and she lived out the rest of her life at the Iroquois Lodge in Ohsweken, Ontario. Her physical body may have let her down, but her ever so keen mind remained bright and alert until the day she died. During her stay in the nursing home, she kept busy by helping with mending clothing – never one to throw anything away that a patch here or there couldn't take care of. I don't know how, but my very private aunt was talked into occasionally announcing the daily events on the public address system. This was so unlike her, but it was sweet to see the twinkle in her eyes when she just causally told us what she did that morning. Another challenge, as usual, she met.

I remember the day that I visited my aunt after she suffered a heart attack and was in recovery; she was so angry. When I asked her why it happened, she said, "Because I'm ready to go." She might have been ready to go, but was I ready to let her go? No, I wasn't – not from her first heart attack. I couldn't even begin to think what life would be like without her. With every weakening of her body, I could see how selfish I was and I slowly realized that her time was coming. On March 14, 1986, at the age of 88, when asked if she would be coming down to the dining room for breakfast, she replied, "No, I can't today. John is coming for me," and shortly after, that very day, he did come for her.

The healing process took a long time. No more Christmas dinners at her table with delicious homemade food, no more conversations, no more sitting and laughing in the big kitchen while visiting relatives were cajoled into playing their guitars, banjos and fiddles, that, coincidentally, they just happened to bring with them. No more just sitting with the summer breeze blowing through the house, no more summer vacations with restful sleep at night tucked in under her homemade quilts. All the tangibles were gone, but one intangible can never be taken from me: the memory of my hero, Aunt Eva.

I have some very lovely items left to me by my aunt, but I think the best one is her bible. It was a birthday gift from her mother and father, given to her in 1922. Some pages were highlighted with bookmarks and several had a four-leaf clover pressed between them, which her keen eyes spied in the lawn. There were some of her handwritten notations about Hades and Paradise and a faded cutout entitled, "Something To Do," which stated, "Read over, thoughtfully, the Ten Commandments." I was about to put the bible down, but I flipped through it one more time and noticed that I missed something: taped in the bible and dated July, 1978, was a note in my Aunt's handwriting. It said:

My Darling Marlene

I shall pass through this world but once. Any good thing that I can do, or any kindness that I can share with others, let me not defer or neglect it, for I shall not pass this way again.

Love, Aunt Eva

Yes, indeed, there are wonderful heroes who put their lives on the line to save another, and then there is my hero. Did my painting depict a hero to you? How many of the bible's teaching could you count in my painting? Love thy neighbour, waste naught, want naught, do unto others… sharing, teaching, companionship, strength in the face of adversity. Just look around you today and see how many unsung heroes you can find. Heroes like my hero: My Aunt (Cora) Eva Baptiste.

••••

ALEXIS MACDONALD SETO

Alexis Macdonald Seto was born in Edmonton, Alberta in 1958. Her ancestry is Métis (Cree and French) on her mother's side and Irish and Scottish on her father's side. Her mother, Blanche Macdonald, was an entrepreneur, a political person and an artist who was active in many First Nations causes and organizations. Alexis grew up witnessing her mother's activities and absorbed and became involved in many of them. In 1987, Alexis received her mothers' Kwak'wala name, Qasalas, meaning a place for walking, from the Sewid family of Campbell River, British Columbia.

Alexis has a Bachelor of Fine Arts degree from the Emily Carr Institute of Art and Design and creates photo-based art, which reflects her personal and cultural history. Her art book, *Let's find out About Indians*, was recently purchased by the University of British Columbia Museum of Anthropology for their permanent collection.

Her greatest source of pride, pleasure and inspiration are her two daughters, Kaya and Isa.

Doreen Jensen –
Journey With a Cultural Activist/Artist

I first met Doreen Jensen in 1985, when I was a student in art school. She was gathering information and preparing to write, *Robes of Power: Totem Poles on Cloth*, a text about the history and contemporary use of the Northwest Coast button blanket. She needed a photographer for her book, someone who would travel around the province with her and take photos of the blanket makers, their families and their communities. As she interviewed me for the job, I remember thinking that she must be more than a little obsessed with this project, wanting to set out in her tiny little car with two people (a researcher was also hired) that she barely knew on a shoe string budget. In addition, the trip involved traveling to remote areas of the province in the middle of winter. What an adventure!

Our interview took place at the Vancouver Friendship Centre and, as we talked, I grew more and more impressed with this soft-spoken woman, whose knowledge of the Northwest Coast culture was vast and whose vision involved bringing recognition to an art form that spoke about family and cultural histories, but was not widely acknowledged. I remember thinking that, although her voice was soft, her words were powerful. I recognized in Doreen, the qualities of a visionary and, in some ways, she reminded me of my mother, the kind of person who can take a seed of an idea and grow it into a multi-faceted project by gathering the right pieces and people together in order to create something of lasting impact.

What I didn't know at the time of out meeting was that I was about to enter into the saddest and most difficult time of my life, as my mother was diagnosed with terminal cancer. Looking back now, I can see that it was no small coincidence that Doreen was coming into my life at the same time that my mother was beginning her transition over to the spirit world. A strong female role model was leaving and another was entering.

I did end up doing most of the photography for *Robes of Power* and, although I was not able to complete the project due to my mother's illness, I had met an important person in my life and began a learning process that has never stopped.

Today Doreen is a mentor, a friend and a cultural role model for me. Acknowledgement, respect and recognition: these are the traditional ways of being and concepts that she was raised with. Through knowing Doreen, I have learned to acknowledge and respect all my cultural sides and to continue to learn about my family – both my mother's Métis history and my father's Irish and Scottish history. She reminds me that there's always a balance, always two sides to the coin. You must respect all sides of where you come from. She has influenced my thinking, encouraged me along the art-making path, and generously offered ideas and connections that have contributed to who I am today as a woman and an artist.

I have a goal to write the story of my mothers' life and Doreen has encouraged me to complete this goal. She informs me in her gentle, yet persuasive way, that the stories of our lives and our ancestors are important to record and to share in our authentic voices and that it is my responsibility, but also my honour, to write my mother's story. I often hear Doreen's words in the back of my mind, "Just do it, just begin. Put a piece of paper in your bra and every time you get an idea, pull it out and write it down!"

I admire the work that she has accomplished as an artist, as a cultural activist and as a human being. She has challenged typical academic thinking that sometimes attempts to define First Nations art and culture with labels of art and craft, traditional and contemporary. Doreen has been called both a contemporary and a traditional artist, yet I know that she makes no real distinction between these two labels. Her work weaves the past into the present, and vice versa.

Her latest work, part of a recent group exhibition at the Surrey Art Gallery, is an example of this modernist thinking and contemporary approach. Titled *W'ilgyet's Journey*, the work is a human-sized installation depicting a traditional Gitxsan House front and an enlarged page from the accompanying hand bound pop-up book. By revisiting stories that she grew up listening to as a child, Doreen's art book draws us into the world of Gitxsan mythologies and allows us to experience

Gitxsan culture through the accessibility of the pop-up concept.

Doreen has taught me to ask the universe for what is needed, whether it's money to pay the bills, good health for family and myself, or just a close parking spot, and to always remember to respectfully give thanks. As she moves forward on her creative journey with intelligence, wisdom and humour, she inspires me to do the same – and I do remember to thank the universe for bringing such a wonderful friend, role model and mentor into my life.

••••

MONECA SINCLAIRE

Moneca Sinclaire is Newyoywak (Cree) and originally from Northern Manitoba. Her spiritual name is Kewatin Nootim Eskwew (North Wind Woman). She is currently completing a doctorate in Adult Education at the Ontario Institute for Studies in Education and is a mother of a five-year-old child. Her doctorate is entitled *Urban Aboriginal Peoples and their Stories of Diabetes* and part of the thesis will be presented as a radio documentary to honour oral traditions. In addition to education, she tries different art forms such as painting (in many media), writing and beading. Both her education and her art focus on the assertion of Aboriginal world views.

One day in 1992, while I was in Opasquiak Cree Nation in Manitoba I went to visit my Kookum (on my father's side) in Mooselake at the end of the day. Our talk was good. She told me of the pain she was feeling having outlived her first life long partner, Benjamin, as well as her son Phillip. As my Kookum spoke, I could feel the sadness in that moment lifting away. She thanked me for taking the time to listen to "this old lady talk for nothing." I have known my Kookum to endure many other ordeals; throughout which she keeps the smile on her face and is delighted by a person's effort to say "Tansi" to her. She has always, as far back as I can recall, told me and the other grandchildren that we are the ones that keep her living. She wants to live to 100 years old and she is 97 today. After visiting her that night, I went back to my hotel and wrote about how I felt sitting with my Kookum.

My Kookum

Kookum whose life has seen many changes
The lines tell a story of days gone by
Hardships and enduring pain of loved ones gone
To outlive your life partner and then your child
Kookum, I experienced your joy despite the pain

When I visit you a smile crosses your face
You know me as "Joe's daughter"
I am one of your hundreds of grandchildren
Always a cup of tea ready
Kookum, your welcome is genuine

I leave you with arms full
Sandwiches made for my return trip

A picture given of family members
Stories told of days gone by
Kookum, you are in my prayers and thoughts

I have always been so proud of my Kookum. She had 22 children, over 100 grandchildren and has never made any one of us feel unwelcome. Despite living in the 1920s with no running water or electricity, she has always seen the bright side of life. She laughs about her life of hardship and says that she would not trade the life she lived for anything. She has enjoyed each day and each new grandchild, great-grandchild, great-great grandchild, as well as two great-great-great grandchildren. The one thing about my Kookum that I will always carry with me is that she always has a smile. Ekosani!

••••

GLORIA OKENYNAN-SUTHERLAND

Gloria Okenynan-Sutherland is 31 years of age from the Samson Cree nation in Hobbema, Alberta. Currently, she is a second year student at the Centre for Indigenous Theatre in Toronto. It has always been her dream to perform in the arts so that she can share her story and the stories of others.

Spirit of the Wa'pus

*Wa'pus (rabbit)
*Hai-Hai (thank you)
*Gokum (grandmother)
*Cree (Neheywok)
*Nokumnow (my grandmother)

I can still feel the pain I experienced at the age of nine; uncomfortably sitting, sore-covered in bumps and bruises from head to toe, dumbfounded and numb to the words that would change my life forever: "You are coming to live with me now, you are coming home."

My initial reactions were shock and fear. I lowered my head, shame threatening to overcome me, but my spirit seeped relief for my prayers had been answered, although not in the way I had anticipated. At a young age, I had asked the Great Spirit to take me back to the spirit world so I wouldn't feel this pain and continue to suffer like a wounded wa'pus in a snare.

During those years, the Great Spirit had heard me after all. I believe he waited until I was ready and then sent me an angel, an angel that possessed the key of love to unlock and release me from the chains of violence and torment, which seized my spirit. This angel was my gokum, Doreen Rabbit-Auger.

She unconditionally took me into her heart and home, welcomed me as if I was one of her daughters. Upon my arrival she started to teach me the language, culture and traditions of the Neheywok, which have been passed down from generation to generation. Many compare their family tree to an oak tree. I think of mine as the majestic redwood, for that is how great we are as Neheyw's and other First Nations. My gokum did have children but they had matured and branched off bearing fruits of their own. When I arrived, she was already raising two other children to whom I was related. They were my first cousins and together we lived as a family, our medicine wheels turning in unison. Although we had our trials and tribulations, my gokum would always be there to reassure us that our difficulties were just part of a learning process. In our teepee, she was the fire keeper.

My gokum was held in high respect, from the elderly to the youngest of children in many different communities. She was a traditional healer and a guidance counselor at a local high school on a neighboring reserve. She was a kind, considerate woman, full of humour and she held the gift of unselfishness, for she was constantly providing for others. She was an open-minded person, who let us exercise our freedom of choice. When I wanted to explore other faiths, she encouraged me without question or judgment and allowed us to attend an annual Christian bible camp.

She instilled knowledge that could not be taught in our local schools: how to survive and thrive healthily off the land, the ability to heal our sick with herbs that Mother Earth so generously provided for us, and to hunt in the wilderness and honour and respect the animal spirits that sacrificed their worldly existence to us to provide our food, clothing and shelter. She taught us not to waste or misuse the gifts we had been given and to always give thanks to the Great Spirit for graciously bestowing blessings mankind could not grant. Most importantly, my gokum taught me to always give back twice as much as I received.

She was very tolerant, for there were occasions when we were rambunctious and extremely foolish, as all children are during their stages of adolescence. However, if we crossed the line and disobeyed, she would not let it go unnoticed and would most definitely enforce discipline as she saw fit.

Before I came to live with my gokum, I couldn't laugh or be like other children. I stayed behind invisible walls and was afraid to draw attention to myself. My gokum was very patient with me and helped to release me from my confinement by guilt, ridicule, low self-esteem and shame. In turn, she planted seeds that replaced the endless secrets that I had nurtured for so long. And so began the cultivation of a garden that so richly grows: modesty, empathy, respect, honesty, patience and serenity I now tend row by row.

She always wanted the best for me: education, success, and fulfilment in all my endeavors. She always told me to continue to challenge myself and to continue to trek onward because, even though I may wear my moccasins thin, I have enough material to mend them. She taught me not to look or dwell in the past, but to learn from it. She reminded me that, although my spirit will become weary and tired from the obstacles that I meet, I must put my faith and trust in the Great Spirit as I ask for the unselfish courage to conquer the mountain that stands before me and to relish in the beauty of all life. One day, I shall gain the wisdom and the voice of an eagle to sing the songs of my ancestors while soaring the heavens.

All creations of this world must come to an end. It still saddens me that my gokum no longer accompanies us here on Mother Earth. The Great Spirit called her back to the spirit world in my teenage years, but her smile still frequents my memory. Her laughter and teachings chime softly in my ears. She now looks upon and prays for me when I am weak and distraught. She dances with our ancestors in celebration of my triumphs and achievements.

I will always remember the very last words she spoke to me before she departed Mother Earth so suddenly: "Keep the house clean and listen to your elders." Keep the house clean: a reminder to weed my garden. Listen to your elders: continue to seek wisdom.

This poem came to me when I felt powerless and defeated by worldly stress; I truly believe that it was my gokum's spirit reassuring me.

O Little Warrior

You speak but no-one listens

You cry, they tell you to shut up
You act up for attention and all you get is a beating
You try your hardest to gain a friend and all you get is rejection
Feeling empty and loveless you weep yourself to sleep
Asking the Great Spirit to take you away
For you are without soul and lost with no direction

I prayed for you also…
The day you arrived on Mother Earth
I asked the Gisi-Manitow to send the eagle spirit
To guide you on your journey and wrap his wing
Around your fragile frame to shield and fill you
With love and tenderness.
To grant you strength from the bear spirit
So when people cross your path
To deceive and misuse your trust
May you strike back with force, not vengefully
But intellectually and from the heart

O' Little Warrior
The tears you cry shall not be of shame
But of growth that join the river of life.
The words you speak are full of curiosity
And thirst for knowledge:

They shall never be shunned.

Gisi-Manitow gave you many gifts:
It is up to you to use them. May you go into the four directions and return
many moons and seasons later
to share your experiences and wisdom
with our people.

••••

PATRICIA LENA TEICHERT

Patricia is a 67-year old Ojibwe woman who was born on the Long Plain Reserve in Manitoba. She spent most of her childhood living apart from her family and community of origin as she attended two Indian residential schools in Manitoba. One school was Protestant and the other was Catholic. Her first internment at the Portage la Prairie Protestant Indian Residential School lasted 10 years, while her second period of confinement at the Sandy Bay Catholic Indian Residential School lasted less than 18 months.

A few years later, she married an Ojibwe man from the Sandy Bay Indian Reserve, who managed to escape internment in a residential school. At the time of their union, they were both teenagers and, later in life, were blessed with five children.

BIOGRAPHY

CHILDHOOD

My story starts in early childhood, when my mother died giving birth to my brother when I was 20 months old. Shortly after his birth, my baby brother perished due to the lack of medical care. This tragedy was compounded by the extreme hardships brought on by the Depression in 1936 and these two events were key reasons for my placement in a residential school.

DOCUMENTS

According to the documents, I was two years and three months old when my father put me in school. For that reason alone, I have the distinction of being the youngest child ever enrolled in the residential school system, which, believe me, does not instil any level of pride.

ARRIVAL AND NAME CHANGE

The date that my father placed me in Portage La Prairie Indian Residential School happened to fall on Saint Patrick's Day, March 17, 1937. Due to my arrival on that day, the school principal, who was an ordained minister, decided to change my name from Lena to Patricia. He baptized me with this new name and, eventually, my name was shortened to Patsy.

Back home, everyone knows me as Patsy; I never knew my real name was Lena. It wasn't until I was an adult and tried to apply for my birth certificate that I discovered that I was not in the records under the name Patricia. It was then that

I learned that my mother had registered me as Lena.

ABANDONMENT

After my father placed me in school, he left and didn't come back to see me until 1943. I was eight years old by that time. He wore an army uniform when he came to see me and I remember not feeling any kinship towards him. The first visit was very awkward and I recall keeping my head down all through the visit, not uttering a word.

On the second visit he told me that he was going to take me from the Boak family, who took care of me during the holidays and school breaks since I was two, and place me with my paternal grandparents. This news troubled me at the time.

I didn't see much of my father after that second visit because, shortly after, he was shipped overseas. Before he left, however, he visited the Boak farm during the summer holiday and removed me from their care. I was then placed with my paternal grandparents on the Long Plain Reserve.

THE BOAK FAMILY

The Boak's were an elderly couple of English and Scottish descent. Their daughter, Jenny, was the Laundry Supervisor at the Portage La Prairie Indian Residential School. While at the school, Jenny grew attached to me from the start and asked the principal if she could take me with her to the family farm on the weekends and during the holidays. Their farm was about ten miles from the school. Those visits became a regular practice and I spent two months each year on the Boak farm, from the ages of two to eight years.

They were a very kind couple that nurtured me with love and affection. I was showered with toys and pretty clothes. Regretfully, upon my return after two months of loving care at the Boak's, I was subjected to abusive practices at the residential school.

THE EFFECTS OF PRIMARY CONDITIONING

The reality of being placed in residential school at an early age, during the period of life when all children form their first impressions, is that my state of being or conditioning took many turns over the years.

The residential school taught me to devalue everything connected to my culture and imposed different values and cultural standards. Sometimes these messages were imparted in a brutal manner and led me to believe that I was a heathen and that my Native language had no value and should not be spoken. All traces of my identity and history were removed.

ASHAMED

By the time I was eight, my mind was already conditioned to feel shame. My thoughts and feelings were established by the nature of my surroundings. The residential school taught me self-hate and punished me for being who I was. The concept I had of myself was shameful for who I was and for my culture.

SCHOOL ENDS

It was June 30, 1947 when I was 12 years old that my institutional confinement ended at Portage La Prairie Indian Residential School. Following that, I spent a full year at home with my paternal grandparents. Unknowingly, that one year changed my life. It was the beginning of a journey to find myself and to reconnect with my Ojibwe culture.

INJUSTICES

The injustice of forced internment, the loss of culture, the deprivation of family connections and the total omission of a fair and equitable education seriously damaged many First Nations people. Culture is what sustains and provides the strength to prevail. In today's society, knowledge gives power. As a mature woman, I knew I had inner strength, but academically, I was unsure of myself. The process of regaining my self-assurance developed step-by-step, in gradual stages. The final stage resulted in an awakening of self and in the discovery of my greatest role model.

FINDING A ROLE MODEL

This final stage came about later in life. My belief is that inner strength is inherited, but it wasn't clear to me where I inherited the will to prevail. The point of realization happened when I began writing my biography.

When I started putting the words to paper about my grandmother, a moment of truth was revealed. I started to cry. The tears wouldn't stop. I cried and cried. Why was I crying about my grandmother? I recalled that I wasn't even her favorite grandchild. It was at that moment when I realized how she had a major influence on me and that she was my greatest role model. It brought back memories of my grandmother who was a spiritual healer and traditional herbalist. For many years, I had forgotten and buried that knowledge about her deep in the back of my mind.

BEING DISRESPECTFUL

When I reflect on my behavior and the attitude I displayed towards my grandmother as a child, I understand why I acted that way. My resentment was directly related to the indoctrination I received at the institution. I can recall how I felt at that age. I was eight-and-a-half, and just arrived from 'The Land of

Plenty,' the white world I was raised in. My father had just removed me from the Boak's and placed me with my paternal grandparents before he was shipped off to war.

INDOCTRINATION

In my childish mind I viewed my grandmother as someone from the distant past. Her manner of dress was a reminder of those times long past. She wore traditional Ojibwe moccasins, the kind with pointed toes and wrap-around ankle flaps.

She was accustomed to wearing floral design ankle length skirts. Her hair was braided and covered with a black babushka that was tied behind her head. She was from a world that the classroom history books mentioned and depicted as inferior and primitive. This is what I was taught to believe as a child and taught to be ashamed of.

My grandmother was different. She was from a unique past that could never be relived. She was someone who couldn't possibly relate to me or understand my concerns. She was far behind the times and came from a different era. What could this woman teach me that I had not already learned in school? She couldn't read or write, except for Ojibwe syllabics. She didn't live in the white world I just came from, where everything was plentiful and where being accepted was as natural as the air we breathe. The communication gap between us was enormous. I believe the distance I felt towards her came from the indoctrination I received from the educators at the Indian Residential School. I do not place any blame on the Boak family because they never ridiculed my race.

As a child, I can remember my feelings towards my grandmother; I would think, "What right did she have to order me around? She didn't raise me. Nor did she roll out the red carpet to make me fell welcomed when I first arrived." In my childish mind I viewed her as "insignificant" because she was a 'nobody,' "peculiar" because of her manner of dress, "inarticulate" because she spoke broken English, "ignorant" because she was illiterate, and "mean" because she made me work hard. I thought she was just a meddling old woman who cared only about getting the chores done. "Work and earn you keep" was her motto. Yes, I believed, slavery was alive and well at my grandmother's house. I wanted to play and goof off, but idleness was never acceptable to her. So where was the justice? Little did I know that I had many lessons to learn.

MY AWAKENING

When I matured as a woman I came to realize the profound influence my grandmother had on me. Through her actions and the firm upbringing I received during the time I lived with her, the way I viewed myself as an Aboriginal woman was changed. To seek solace in matters of the soul, I often find myself reverting back to her teachings during these profound moments. Yes, my grandmother left me with a legacy of life experiences. Many lessons that were of value and beneficial throughout the years. Some examples of her remarkable integrity that stand out include her work ethic: she believed that hard work was "the stepping stone for self pride." She was the perfect example of an industrious, hard-working woman, skilled in numerous tasks and proficient at earning her own money. She was totally adept in the rules of survival, especially in the woods.

Her ability to share with others was her greatest asset. She was one of the last women I know who truly believed in following the customs of the Ojibwe culture, which was the practice, or art, of giving and sharing. Her monthly pension went towards feeding many households. Every Sunday we had visitors, many of who were families with children and going through financially difficult times. Every child and her grandchild received a special treat. I recall that Sundays were the busiest for me because my job was to bring in wood, haul water, and peel potatoes. Every person who came to visit was fed.

My grandmother was very modest. She never mentioned a word about her accomplishments or achievements; boasting was not acceptable in Ojibwe culture.

Her responsibility as a grandmother was remarkable. She brought up 30 or more grandchildren and raised two of her sisters' daughters. Most of the children she had in her care were brought to her when they were ill. She would nurse them back to health at her home until they were well enough to return to their parents. During my stay with her, she had five children in her care.

As a midwife, she was called upon to deliver over 100 babies, most of them from the Long Plain Reserve. Many were her grandchildren and great-grandchildren.

As a wife, she treated her husband with respect and always had his meals ready on time. I never heard her raise her voice to my grandfather, but when she was displeased with him, she gave him the silent treatment. That stressed my grandfather so, to pacify the situation, he would follow her around like a little puppy.

Her subdued silence: she had the capacity to refrain from voicing her opinion and to remain neutral when my grandfather got agitated, venting all his frustrations at her. She would let him continue until he dispensed with his angry tone. During his state of annoyance she would acknowledge him with a "hmm," which was generally understood to mean, "I hear you" or "I understand." Later when things were calmer, she would discus the matter with him.

Her dutiful role as a mother: She built strong bonds and maintained her contact with each on of her children. She sustained her relationship with them and their children. Every grandchild was precious in her eyes.

She provided advice and support when called upon. Her presence as a parent was constant. She defended and protected her family intensely. As a mother-in-law, she was treated with great respect.

Her unbridled show of love: her capacity to allow her feelings to surface when my father, George, was severely injured by a tractor, I heard her desperate wails and stressful cries, "hi, hi Gozis; hi, hi Gozis" (meaning oh my son, oh my son), which resound in my memory and will always remain embedded there. I watched my grandfather calm her so that he could lessen the trauma and deal with the matter at hand. To relieve stress in matters of extreme tragedy or the loss of a loved one, Ojibwe women dealt with their losses by wailing and by applying hands-on support among one another.

Her strength and calm demeanor: she displayed tremendous courage one day when a messenger came to our door to tell my grandmother that her son, Donald, was lying injured on the side of the road about two miles away. Apparently, the horse my uncle was riding tripped and fell and landed directly on my uncle's leg. Donald was about 14. My grandfather was away at the time so I was with my grandmother when she went to pick Donald up in the wagon; there were no vehicles on the reserve at that time. The messenger and my grandmother lifted Donald onto the wagon and, throughout the trip home, Donald cried out in agony whenever we encountered a rut in the road. My grandmother would stop to comfort and reassure him that we were almost home. I watched my grandmother pray silently that day. Her face was strained, but composed, throughout the ordeal.

Her unswerving faith: her prayers and faith never eluded her while her sons were away at war. Many times I watched her gaze out the window and say a prayer, asking the Creator to keep her sons safe, and to send them home soon.

Her endless generosity: it seemed that her sole purpose in life was to feed everyone and to share her wealth, as meagre as it was. The fruit she canned all summer was shared with her visitors or given away as gifts to friends and relatives. She canned everything from wild berries to store bought pig heads. Each time she returned from a trip, she would count her sealers to ensure that the children didn't help ourselves without asking her.

THE COAT

I remember one incident regarding a black winter coat. The coat was well made and in excellent condition, which made it all the more valuable. The box cut was in style during that period and the quality of the material was of a high grade. Whenever my grandmother wasn't around, I would try it on. I could see it was a perfect fit for me. It hung on a coat rack where everyone could see it.

Every time my aunts and cousins came to visit they would try it on and beg to buy it from my grandmother, but my grandmother always answered with, "No, I'm not selling it, I'm saving it for someone special." It hung on that rack for more than three months, then one day in the late fall, in the presence of some visitors and relatives, she brought the coat down and presented it to me. But not until she gave me a lecture on the virtues of "the work ethic," which was her way of spelling out why I deserved this gift and what I had accomplished to receive it.

Deep down, I was the happiest girl on the earth because, on numerous occasions, I asked my father to buy me a winter coat. He never responded, not even with a "maybe." This gift provided great relief for me, knowing that I didn't have to be ashamed of going out in public in an old coat.

I still had to overcome the embarrassment of wearing boy's rubber gumboots, however. I thought, "Oh well, maybe I can manage to hide them some way or another; maybe cover them up with a scarf when I sit down or hide them behind some object if I have to stand in a spot."

HER TRADITIONAL BELIEFS

My grandmother was a very traditional Ojibwe woman. She followed teachings and practiced the customs of her heritage. She took great pride in carrying out those teachings, teachings that were passed down from the ancient ones of many generations past.

Her beliefs survived the invasion of Christianity, the restrictions of the reserve life, the removal of her children, the assimilation enforced on her children by the residential school system, the cultural genocide of her people, the alcoholism, the diseases, and the monetary entrapment, which affected the values of her people. Every possible method was utilized to eradicate the ancient Ojibwe teachings, but still, she never wavered. She remained steadfast in her beliefs to the end.

For me, she represented the strength, sensitivity, and dignity of Ojibwe women. She was truly the one and only traditional Ojibwe woman I had the privilege of knowing.

••••

PENNY 'EMILY' YOUNGREEN

Penny 'Emily' Youngreen is an artist, illustrator and writer living in Southeastern British Columbia. She serves as a volunteer advisory committee member of Lower Columbia River All First Nations Council, a support and advocacy organization for First Nations people living off reserve.

Born in the United States of Métis and Hawaiian ancestry and raised by her Hawaiian Grandparents, she retells the stories learned at her Grandmother's kitchen table long ago.

Tutu's Gift

When I was eight years old, I went to live with my mother's mother, Maila, or as we called her, Grandma Louise, although it's never been explained to anyone how or why it was that her name changed.

Every morning before school, my grandmother would pin holy medals of the Virgin Mary, St. Christopher, and the blessed son Jesus to my undershirt with a big safety pin. She would then carefully tie a few coins into a handkerchief for me to buy a little something to have with my lunch from the tiny Chinese market that was kitty corner from my schoolyard.

One day I asked her why she insisted on tying the coins into the handkerchief since I had my own purse: a green plastic one with a shiny copper coin glued to the front of it with my name printed in large block letters above the coin. This is the story she told me.

No matter which direction six-year-old Maila looked, there was nothing to see but rolling waves, nothing but ocean from horizon to horizon. It had been days since she waved goodbye to her tutu and her aunties, Kamoohila, Hattie and Poepoe. They stood on the planked pier placing flower leis and maile garlands on the shoulders of her little family and tossing more after them onto the water as the ship slid slowly away toward the open sea. If she closed her eyes she could see Tutu Pokii standing there still, tears streaming down her cheeks as her mother's hand tightened around her own small hand. Maila, her mother Kaehukai, and little brother Keoki, stood still and silent as statues at the ship's rail until their kupuna whaine, their aunties, and the shores of Ohau vanished beneath the curving edge of the sea.

Jacinto, Maila's father, had gone below decks shortly upon embarking. He was always looking for a good game of Pinochle and had heard, before even purchasing their tickets, that this ship's first mate was a gambling man with a long record of losses. How fortunate he was to get passage on this ship where there was always a lively game going.

Jacinto had worked in the cane fields like his father before him, but neither the work nor the low pay was to his fancy. He decided that his future and that of his family lie across the sea on the mainland. There, he was told, was opportunity and fortune. No more slaving in the sugar cane. Good jobs were a dime a dozen and so he could pick and choose.

Maila spent the idle days aboard the ship trying to imagine this new land the ship was steaming toward. Would the wind be soft and warm? Would the trees sway in the wind and would there be the same clear, warm blue ocean to swim in? Would she be able to pick opehe off the beach with her little brother? Most of all, who would be there to greet them if all her family was left behind? What would the people be like?

She had in her possession all the pennies her Tutu had given her on the day of her departure. Tutu had wrapped more pennies than Maila could count into her Grandfather Iokua's large white handkerchief and had tied them securely with a double knot. Pennies and the memory of kupuna kane Tutu's sweet love for her were held there in the hanky pouch for he was not able to leave the cane fields that day to be on the dock to offer his tears or place leis upon the waters.

It was a heavy and fair sized bundle that all but filled both of her hands. When she wasn't helping look after Keoki, she would tug at the knots until the handkerchief opened to reveal the pennies. Shiny coppers and dull coppers and even some that were a most amazing green. It was good to run her fingers over the pennies that her Tutus had given her. She would carefully gather them into a pile in the middle of the kerchief and then retie them as her grandmother had.

Maila sat, legs stretched out on the deck before her, absorbed in admiration of the pennies glinting in the sun on the white altar of her grandfather's hanky. The first mate, fresh from loosing another card game and smelling of cheap whisky, walked toward her weaving slightly and stood swaying against the ocean's roll, casting his shadow across her and stealing the sunshine that glorified her treasure.

"What's that you got there little kanaka girl? Pennies? What you gonna do with them pennies? Nobody buys things with pennies where you're goin' little kanaka girl. Hasn't anyone ever told you, the streets are paved with gold? Only poor people spend pennies," he snorted. "Only POOR people got pennies," he said emphasizing 'poor' with a sneer as if it were an affliction or a smelly disease. He staggered off, leaving her gazing at the pennies. No longer did the shine. They sat there on the slightly soiled handkerchief, suddenly dull, all lustre gone.

Maila had no idea what the word meant, but understood it must mean something truly horrible. She wondered, "Why would my beloved Tutus give me something so horrible?" They must not have known how shameful and horrible poor is, as there was never any question that her grandmother and grandfather loved her beyond life itself and would not knowingly give her something that was bad. It didn't make sense, but the last thing Maila would ever do, if she could help it, was bring shame on her ohana (family), least of all to her respected and loved kupunas. From her birth, she had been told that hers was a proud ohana. She was descended from Chief Hoolue, a great chief and warrior who fought along side King Kamahamaha and whose ahupua'a (a land of division usually going from the top of the mountain to the sea) was large and powerful. Maila, only six years upon the earth, resolved in that moment that she would not be the one to bring shame to her family.

She gathered the pennies one last time, tied them up, tearfully got back to her feet and moved resolutely to the ship's rail. With trembling lips and held back sobs, she tossed her Tutu's gift into the sea. Unlike those fragrant maile wreaths and flowers at her departure, the pennies fell beneath the foam in less than an instant. This was not a simple thing, to throw away a gift given in love by your grandmother and grandfather, but this was to be Maila's gift to her Tutus and all her ohana and it was a painfully courageous act for a little girl.

Two days later they saw land. San Francisco was the destination for the creaking old freighter. They had been seeing smoke on the horizon off the bow for the last day and a half. The smoke became thicker and blacker as they neared land. The stench of it made everyone's nose wrinkle and look at each other with a puzzled expression. "What is this place we are going to?" her mother asked, "it smells like Hell!"

Later that day they pulled into San Francisco harbor, or what remained of it. The city was in flames; the year was 1906. The great earthquake occurred while they were still at sea only days before and now it looked as if the entire city was burning. Every hill was a column of flames. The fire had a voice of its own that could be heard above all else and in that voice could be heard the clanging of alarm bells on the horse drawn fire engines and the screams of those fighting the flames or trying to escape them.

The ship's captain and his first mate came to stand beside them to stare at the horror before them. The captain was the first to speak, "We'll have to take you up the coast a bit and drop you folks up there. Can't leave you here even if we wanted to."

The first mate looked down at Maila grasping the rail, her eyes tearing from the acrid smoke and staring into a waking nightmare. He spoke softly to her, sobered by the vision they shared, "Good thing you got them pennies girl, your family is gonna need every red cent. Looks like everyone's poor now."

My mother told me when I was born that she asked my grandmother to choose a name for me and she chose Penny, not Penelope, but Penny. And now, so many years later, I understand. It was my Tutu's gift.

••••

MERLIN HOMER

Merlin Homer is mixed blood Salish and Mohawk on her mother's side and Russian on her father's side. She works as a counselor, a visual artist, and sometimes, a singer. She has participated in over 35 group and solo exhibitions dating back to 1965, including many performances of traditional music with the Anishnawbe Quek Singers and Sweetgrass City Singers as well as opera with the Toronto Opera Repertoire. She has been a guest lecturer on Native culture at York University and has taught both Native Literature and the Bridging Course for Native Women at Atkinson College, York University. She is grateful to belong to a culture that understands and accepts the kinds of experiences that underlie her paintings and about which she has written here.

Learning to Live with Death:
The Example of my Mother, Jean Homer

My mother, Jean, lived her entire life under a death sentence. By her love for, and wonder at, the world, as well as the 'iron will' she associated with being a Native woman, she lived three months past her 81st birthday.

Jean's heart was severely damaged by rheumatic fever when she was in her teens. From her 20s on, she also suffered from degeneration of her lungs. By the time she died, her doctor explained to me, it was simply a matter of both organs failing at the same time.

Jean loved to be out on the land. Her state of mind, and thus her apparent level of health and energy, always improved remarkably when she was on the land and, the way things worked in our family, this was usually when she was really mad at my father. When they made up, something she also really liked, at least for a while, she came home and was less herself, less able to act decisively on her own behalf. She seemed to be living for others. At the lowest of these times – for this way of living is a recipe for burnout in the healthiest of us – she would sometimes speak about wishing to die. I think this was the only way out of the cycle she could imagine when her energy was low.

My happiest memories of my mother are of camping with her. I can see the sun on her brown face, her hair blowing free, her body straight and accepting of the elements. She managed a campsite with joy and ease. Camping by the ocean, we cooked and ate steamer clams that we dug up ourselves. Fortunately, my mother was 'good and angry' at my father a lot of the time.

During her lifetime, with poor health that the doctors were always warning her about (neither I nor my brother would exist if she had listened to them), Jean was realistic and honest about death, and spoke to me about it calmly. I listened. She said being aware that she could die taught her to value each day of her life the best she could; to enjoy it the best she could. Because she had a plan for living her life in the face of death, I received a source of serenity that I am sure has saved my life more than once. As her firstborn, and her daughter, however, through much of my life I have also, too often, imitated the unhappy side of her life – forgetting that my primary responsibility in life is myself and believing that dying and running away are good problem-solving strategies.

Jean died very peacefully, but her teachings about death have not ceased. She died in a hospital room, my father on one side of her, holding one of her hands; my youngest brother Jason on the other side, holding her other hand; and my father talking about the good old times. Her death at this moment was so gentle as to be imperceptible, and it took the two men with her a moment to realize that this was a little rest she was not going to wake up from. Dad and Jason wept. After the removal of Jean's body, Jason stayed behind to pack her belongings.

What Jason told me about packing up Jean's things had a tremendous impact on me. He repeated several times that the room seemed filled with her spirit; that it felt amazingly peaceful and sacred while he emptied the closet and dresser in her room and folded and put away her clothing and belongings. Her belongings were mostly funny things from her children and grandchildren like a Taco Bell New Year's Chihuahua that says, "Happy New Year Amigos," when you press the belly.

Since I am a painter, I began to try to imagine what it would be like to make a painting of the scene. I wrote in a notebook I keep for painting ideas, "A woman has peacefully died in her bed. Her husband and son sit on either side of her. Her spirit fills the space, blessing it." I had no doubt of my brother's story; I believed that she was teaching him, in the very moment of death, to find the blessing in the smallest and simplest tasks. I envied him. I did not realize that teachings for me were still to come.

Although she died in July, Jean's funeral was postponed until September, when it became a memorial service. My father, about six weeks before she died, in his grief and denial, decided to make it up to her. When she died before he could, this desire transformed into quite a large event, entailing quite a lot of money and preparation. Meantime, the other bereaved, being outside the loop of this major event, were left to fend for themselves without a ritualized goodbye.

So it happened, when my wonderful clan sister Evelyn invited me to spend the Tyendinaga pow-wow weekend with her, I went gladly. At Evelyn's insistence, I wore a ribbon dress. The two of us were placed at the back of the Grad Entry parade as elders and I thought, "Here it is, I'm next in line, no one in front of me anymore." Meaning that, in the natural order of things, my generation is the next to go. Dancing slowly and seemingly endlessly in the circle, I felt my mother's presence and her happiness to see me doing this. I began to feel some happiness in myself. As I felt some happiness, her presence became stronger, increasing my dawning sense of joy. The happier I felt, the stronger her presence became; the stronger her presence became, the deeper went my joy. As it continued, I received the teaching that, to do what makes one joyful is to do what is right, what one must.

But the lesson did not end there, and what happened next I will continue to learn from as long as I live. As my mother's presence expanded, on this brilliantly sunny day, I also felt her above me. Looking up, I realized she was the sky, the whole sky. Although I cannot explain this, I understood it with a certainty that has never left me. It took me, when I needed it, outside the Sea Cliff Methodist Church and into the starry sky on the night of her funeral, making it possible for me to sing well the Laudamus Te, the song of praise, that was my assigned part of the evening.

I finally did find my way to paint my mother's death. I call the painting, *She Is the Sky*. Like the circle in which we dance, and all understanding, the painting is round, surrounded in a thin line by the four colors. Because my mother had, in death, come to me as the sky, there are many symbols of the sky in the painting – clouds, stars, sun, and a rainbow separating the upper and lower worlds. Near the bottom are my mother's small, lifeless form and my weeping brother and father. It is discernable that they are in a room with an open window, these forms linear and plain – a hospital room. Around them, passing through the rainbow and filling the sky, is an image of my mother's gentle and embracing spirit. I felt grateful that I had sufficiently done what I love best in life – painting – that I in fact had the skill and experience to create the complex image.

Through death and beyond it, my mother has given me convincing teachings about life and has healed, perhaps, some of the mistaken notions about life that I took from her more troubled times. By honestly sharing with me how she coped with the physical dangers posed by her medical history, I believe she taught me to be calm. Living as long and as lovingly as she did, she taught me the incredible power of will (which she always assured me, as a 'real' Native woman, I had). In death, she bestowed the mystic gift of oneness and individuality, which I know will nourish my mind and soul and life as long as I have them. I know now, without doubt, that it is right to be strong for who and what one is, for joy, and for all things that create joy and beauty in the world – and nothing else.

••••

Visual Artists' Biographies

MERLIN HOMER

See the biography for Merlin Homer in the Short Stories section on page 94.

KATHY AINSLEY

Kathy Ainsley (Seneca/Dutch) is a poet and artist. She is a member of Wordcraft Circle of Native Writers and Storytellers and has worked as an art teacher and for *Mothering Magazine*. She has one son Galen, who is also an artist, and she currently resides in the Santa Cruz Mountains with her husband Harry.

CHRISTI BELCOURT

Christi Belcourt (b. 1966) is a Métis woman who was raised in Ottawa and whose ancestry comes from both the Métis community of Lac St. Anne, Alberta and from Bedford, Nova Scotia. She is a self-taught artist who has been painting since the age of 15.

Like generations of Métis and First Nation artists before her, Christi celebrates the beauty of flowers and plants while exploring their symbolic properties. She creates gorgeous paintings of flowers painted in jewel tones on a monochrome pastel ground. Her paintings possess a smooth, stylized elegance, and each presents an exquisite bouquet, a paean to the botanical world.

Christi is a past recipient of grants from the Canada Council for the Arts, Ontario Arts Council and the Métis Nation of Ontario. In 2001, the Canadian Museum of Civilization acquired a piece entitled *Remembering Batoche* for permanent display within the prestigious First People's Hall in Hull, Quebec.

In addition to her painting, Christi also had a regular column called "Art Beat" in the *Métis Voyageur Newspaper* and has begun the National Métis Arts Registry to create a network for Métis artists.

CARLA GILDAY

Carla Rae Gilday is a Dene artist from Yellowknife, Northwest Territories. She is currently attending the University of Victoria and working towards a degree in Visual Art. She enjoys a variety of art forms, but painting has always been her main creative outlet. The content of her work reflects many stories, dreams and encounters and has always been a powerful form of medicine for her.

MAYA CHRISTINA GONZALEZ

Maya Christina Gonzalez is an award-winning artist, illustrator and educator. Her work is shown primarily throughout the United States, and she is currently working on her 16th children's book. Many of her books are bilingual, English/Spanish and have won numerous awards. Her piece, *The Love That Stains*, graces the recently released double-volume art books: *Contemporary Chicana/Chicano Art, Education and Culture*. Largely self-taught, Maya's work focuses primarily on women and their relationship with the invisible worlds.

MARIA HUPFIELD

Of the Martin clan Wasauksing First Nation, Maria Hupfield is an Anishnaabekwe artist, art educator and Coordinator of 7th Generation Image Makers in Toronto. She holds a Master of Fine Arts in Sculpture from York University and a Bachelor of Arts (Honours) with a major in Art and Art History and minor in Aboriginal Studies from the University of Toronto and Sheridan College. Having grown up on the shores of Georgian Bay, Maria now works and lives in Toronto. At the age of 31, she is a vibrant young artist with a diverse and engaging portfolio of traditional and contemporary work.

Maria has been actively involved with implementing arts initiative programs, with a special interest in education as well as creative cultural arts development for First Nations Communities. She has extensive experience coordinating mural groups and art programs involving youth at-risk and children. Some of the various group shows and exhibitions Maria has participated in include: The Art Gallery of Hamilton, Thunder Bay Art Gallery, Indian Art Centre and the Red Head Gallery.

BARBARA-HELEN HILL

Barbara-Helen Hill is a visual artist and writer living and working on Six Nations of the Grand River. She is a mother and grandmother of two beautiful granddaughters. Helen, as she likes to be called, has just ventured into the fibre arts and is enjoying it tremendously. She has been a painter for a number of years and is now trying her hand at picture quilting, embroidery and using a combination of all in her work. Helen is also the author of *Shaking the Rattle: Healing the Trauma of Colonization*, which is now in its second printing.

BUFFY SAINTE-MARIE

Born on a Cree reservation in Qu'Appelle Valley, Saskatchewan, Buffy Sainte-Marie is an internationally acclaimed singer, songwriter and musician. She made 17 albums of her music, three of her own television specials, spent five years on Sesame Street, scored movies, helped to found Canada's 'Music of Aboriginal Canada' JUNO category, raised a son, earned a Ph.D. in Fine Arts, taught Digital Music as adjunct professor at several colleges, and won an Academy Award Oscar for the song Up Where We Belong.

Buffy Sainte-Marie virtually invented the role of Native American international activist pop star. Her concern for protecting indigenous intellectual property, and her distaste for the exploitation of Native American artists and performers has kept her in the forefront of activism in the arts for 40 years. Presently, she operates the Nihewan Foundation for Native American Education whose Cradleboard Teaching Project serves children and teachers in 18 states.

As a composer, she won an Academy Award in 1982 for the song *Up Where We Belong* as recorded by Joe Cocker and Jennifer Warnes for the film *An Officer and A Gentleman*.

An educator before she was ever known as a singer, Buffy lectures at colleges and civic venues on a wide variety of topics: film scoring, electronic music, songwriting, Native American studies, the Cradleboard Teaching Project, women's issues, and remaining positive amidst tough human realities. She serves as Adjunct Professor in Canada at York University in Toronto and Saskatchewan Indian Federated College in Regina, and in the U.S., was an Evans Chair Scholar at the Evergreen State College in Washington State. She has also taught at the Institute for American Indian Arts in Santa Fe, New Mexico.

BRENDA RAILEY

Brenda Railey is inspired by the people, land and sea of the Pacific. Her background is Pacific Island, and she spent her formative years in Somoa. Her ancestry includes grandparents from Samoa, Tonga and Niue. Her professional background has been primarily within the corporate arena, however, a change of career 10 years ago led Brenda to work in both the traditional and contemporary Pacific Island arts arena. In her current role, she project manages artists in public spaces. Brenda resides in Auckland, New Zealand.

Muse

The Muse of Greek mythology presides over the arts and sciences and this work is a metaphor for the consideration of a Pacific muse. It epitomizes a beautiful Pacific Island woman, Fa'amele Etuale, floating and meditating in the Pacific Ocean on Arorangi Beach in Rarotonga.

DAPHNE ODJIG

Born in 1919, on the Wikwemikong Indian Reserve, Manitoulin Island, Ontario. Daphne Odjig is internationally renowned visual artist with a career spanning over 60 years. She has made a unique and significant contribution to First Nations and to the broader Canadian art world.

Woodland School painter, Odjig has earned some of this nation's most important honours, including the Order of Canada (1986), and honorary degrees from several universities, and many prestigious commissions such as for Ottawa's National Museum of Man. Distinguished among the Woodland school by her expressive and lyric use of the formline, Odjig's work contributed to many of the milestone exhibitions of contemporary Native art throughout the 1970s and 1980s. The subject of multiple biographies, films, plays and documentaries, she co-founded the Professional Native Indian Artists Inc., created Indian Prints of Canada, Inc., the Warehouse Gallery, and taught and consulted for the Society of Canadian Artists of Native Ancestry (SCANA). Odjig is currently a member of the Royal Canadian Academy, and continues to be an inspiration to many young Aboriginal and non-Aboriginal artists and students.

Visual Art

She is the Sky, 2000. Watercolour on paper.

Skywoman, 1998. Oil paint on paper.

CHRISTI BELCOURT

We Are Not Alone, 2002. Acrylic on canvas, 48" x 57"
Permanent collection of the Centre for Traditional Knowledge, Museum of Nature

CHRISTI BELCOURT

Remembering Batoche, 2002. Acrylic on canvas, 48" x 48"

Permanent collection of the Canadian Museum of Civilization

Photograph courtesy of the Canadian Museum of Civilization catalogue no. S20001-4737 Y-Z-138

Elysium Sun Goddess. Acrylic on canvas, 72" x 24".

Soul Sister. Acrylic on canvas, 12" x 24".

Sky Woman Falls into the Millenium, 2002.

Shell Woman

Smoking Prayer

Woman With Peach, 1998.

Tikinaagan, 2000. Installation.

Spirit Catchers, 2000.

Muse

Goddess of the Yellow Moon

Dream Goddess

SANDRA LARONDE

Sandra Laronde hails from the Teme-Augama-Anishnaabe (People of the Deep Water) in Temagami, Ontario and resides in Toronto. As the Founder and Artistic Producer of Native Women in the Arts, Sandra is also an actor, dancer, writer and founding Artistic Director of Red Sky Performance.

In 2004, Sandra was one of 225 Canadians chosen to participate in the *Governor-General's Canadian Leadership* program that celebrates promising leaders making a significant impact on Canada. In the same year, Sandra was also the recipient of Toronto City Council's 2004 *Aboriginal Affairs Award* for her significant contribution towards improving the quality of life for the Aboriginal community of Toronto. She is also listed in the *Canada's Who's Who* that features notable living Canadians.

In 1993, Sandra founded Canada's only organization for First Nations, Inuit and Métis women artists, Native Women in the Arts, which has played a significant role in fostering the careers of thousands of Aboriginal women and female youth. Since 1993, Native Women in the Arts has helped to produce an immense ripple effect of artistic growth, confidence building and proliferation of performing arts, literary arts and publishing, visual arts, and community development projects.

She is published in *Cultures in Transition* (McGraw-Hill), *Chinook Winds* (Banff Centre Press), *Gatherings* (Theytus Books), *Crisp Blue Edges* (Theytus Books), written for CBC Radio, and is currently a play creator in residence at Canadian Stage. She is also a co-editor of *My Home As I Remember* and *Sweetgrass Grows All Around Her*, both published by Native Women in the Arts.

Sandra graduated from the University of Toronto with a Bachelor of Arts (Honours), and studied overseas for one year at the University of Granada in Spain.